1630L

JUMPING *the* NAIL

Eve Bunting

Harcourt Brace & Company

San Diego   New York   London

Requests for permission to make copies of any part of
the work should be mailed to:
Permissions Department,
Harcourt Brace & Company,
6277 Sea Harbor Drive,
Orlando, Florida 32887-6777.

Library of Congress Cataloging-in-Publication Data
Bunting, Eve, 1928–
Jumping the nail/by Eve Bunting.
p.   cm.
When a group of teenagers in a coastal California
community challenge each other to "jump the Nail"—
leap from dangerous cliffs into the ocean—group
pressure and manipulative relationships quickly drive
the game out of control.
ISBN 0-15-241357-X
ISBN 0-15-241358-8 (pb)
[1. Peer pressure—Fiction.]   I. Title
PZ7.B91527Jt   1991
[Fic]—dc20   91-11090

Printed in the United States of America

G F E D C B
S R Q P O N M L K J (pb)

To Diane (one "n")
and Jeannette (two "n's")—
we did not jump

JUMPING
the
NAIL

ONE

IT WAS EARLY and Mom and Dad were still asleep. I called softly to Rusty, our crazy-looking, sausagey dachshund, and opened the front door. He came running on his stumpy legs, long tail swishing with joy, and together we ran out into the morning.

Sometimes June mornings in California are chilly and dank with a fog that billows in from the ocean and doesn't lift till noon. La Paloma is right on the coast, so sometimes the fog hangs around all day. But not this day. It was sunny and warm with blue skies. We ran along the sidewalk, past Rick's Surf Shop, past La Paloma High where I'd graduated last week with the rest of my class. Gardeners were working in front of some new boxy condos with baby-crib–sized balconies and views of the beach.

"Two hundred fifty thousand dollars, fifteen percent down," my mom had told us. Mom knows.

She just got her real estate license and is hoping to make a few of those two-hundred-fifty-thousand-dollar sales.

I never mind Mom talking about housing prices as long as she doesn't start on how she wishes we owned our house instead of renting. "I knew all along we should buy," she tells Dad accusingly. "But here we are, still paying rent, and people making fortunes all around us."

It makes me mad when she gets on to that.

Rusty and I thumped down the wooden steps to the golden, tide-washed beach, empty except for another jogger way in the distance.

The sea was dark with kelp, and the usual sailboats bobbed gently along beyond the mild curl of surf.

I glanced up at the house, huge, glass walled, perched on the edge of the cliff. Mike's house. Maybe he was watching me from one of those windows. He could even have binoculars and he'd see me in my raggedy shorts and my sister Claire's shapeless, washed-out red T-shirt. Why hadn't I worn something decent? I should have remembered those windows.

The jogger was closer to us now. I saw that it was Diane Skoal.

Great, I thought.

Diane had graduated with me. I guess I've known her forever, but we've never been friends. I didn't think we were friends now, though girls, and guys, too, who hadn't known I was alive all through high school had started noticing me these last two months. Because of Mike, of course. Because he'd noticed me. Being Mike's girlfriend was the only thing about me now that was different. Diane had noticed me all right. But given that *she'd* been Mike's girlfriend before he met me, I didn't think she liked me much. Once she'd have run on by. Now she stopped.

"Hi, Dru. Hi, Rusty." She bent to pet him. It was almost funny. Not long ago she probably hadn't known my name. Now she knew the name of my dog! "Sweet doggie," she murmured.

Diane was wearing pink sweats tucked into white socks with pink stripes. Even her running shoes were pink, and her pale blond hair was tied back with a pink ribbon. I sure hoped Mike didn't have his binocs out.

She straightened.

"Are you and Mike going to the Nail this afternoon? I guess everybody's going to be there."

I still wasn't used to being paired with Mike this

way. It made me feel important, but nervous, too. It didn't seem real.

"I'm not sure what we're doing," I said. "Is something happening there?"

"Only that Scooter Navarro's jumping." Diane jogged in place.

"Jumping the Nail? No!" I couldn't believe it. "He's not really going to?"

"He says he is." Diane was talking as if this were just somebody jumping off a diving board or the side of a pool.

"Course, he may chicken out," she said. "But that'll be fun, too."

She stopped jogging, smoothed back her hair, and gave me a quick look. "Do you know yet when you leave for Northwestern?"

"The middle of September," I said.

She bent to straighten a sock that didn't need to be straightened. "Well, nice to get a scholarship. Nice to be a brain. I suppose you won't be back after that till Christmas."

"No."

She half smiled and instantly I understood the question and the half-smile that went with it. Diane and Mike were both going to San Diego State, though Mike would only be there part-time. Still.

They'd be bound to see each other. And I'd be long gone. Diane was dating one of the McInerney twins now. Tom, who played guard on the football team. His twin, Grant, was left tackle. But could Diane really care about Tom McInerney after Mike?

"Well . . ." She waved a cheery hand. "See you at the Nail."

"I don't know," I said, but she was already gone, following her own tracks back along the sand.

I looked up again at Mike's house, the sun behind it, the windows dark and shining. Later in the day the crevices in the cliff beneath it would blaze with scarlet ice plant. El Nido, the nest, it was called, and the name seemed right for it, so high on its perch.

"Two million at least," my mom said. She always sighed at any mention of El Nido. Then Dad would hide behind his newspaper and I'd call Rusty for a run.

Because my mom might have been mistress of El Nido. Mistress of El Nido. The words had a corny ring, like the title of a cheap paperback with a tawdry cover. But it wasn't corny to her. It was a definite might have been. When she was my age she'd dated—"heavily dated," as she called it— Sam Moriarty, Mike's dad. He hadn't been rich then. "But I knew he would be one day," Mom said. "He had ambition." He hadn't become Moriarty Construction yet. Or master of El Nido, either. That came later, when he came back here a year ago and built the house, one of the most remarkable houses around. And now I was dating Sam's son. Not heavily dating, but dating. My mom was overjoyed. "He looks just the way his dad looked at that age," she said dreamily. "Handsome, sexy. History repeating itself." She'd folded her hands in front of her as if she were praying. And maybe she was. "And, Dru, you be smart. You look to your future." Usually she'd add, "I have no regrets, of course. Your dad and I were in love. Are in love. That first time I saw your father at the piano of the Marvue Hotel all thoughts of Sam Moriarty flew right out of my head." Dad's paper would be very still, and behind it he'd be very still, too.

"Well, Dad's doing great, too," I'd say. I'd punch his shoulder or kiss the top of his head. "Manager of the biggest music and musical instrument shop in La Paloma—with the best inventory anywhere."

And sometimes then Mom would chime in, "And still the most popular weekend piano player the Marvue Hotel has." Her words would be fine, but sometimes she'd bite her lips or sigh and the sigh would take the good out of what she'd said.

Sometimes I thought I wanted nothing more to do with Mike Moriarty because of all this history repeating itself stuff. But then, this was Mike, who was not only gorgeous and popular and rich, but nice, too, and friendly to everyone. Who stood up to those off-campus guys when they came over the fence and began picking on Derek Blaine. Mike who was special and who'd noticed me that night and made me special, too.

I was still staring at the house, high on the cliff top. Was their cliff as high as the Nail that Scooter Navarro would jump today? The Nail is almost ninety feet from the top to the surface of the water, and who knows how many feet below that, down, down, down? They say it is bottomless at the Nail's stem, at the place we call the Deep. They say there are caves, dark underwater caves. No one has ever touched bottom. They say there is a car wedged down there with two skeletons in it, a boy and a girl who went over a long time ago. Nobody has ever seen the car, though sometimes, when the tide is really low and you lean far over on the rocks that ring the Deep, there seems to be a red shimmer in the water, a shine that shows itself and is gone.

I could vaguely remember the last time someone had jumped. I guess I'd been in third grade. It was a girl, I remember that. She'd misjudged it somehow and hit the rocks instead of the water and had broken her back. They'd dropped a helicopter in and lifted her on a sling, and just about everyone in La Paloma had lined the Nail, standing well back, watching that swaying sling with the girl in it. I wasn't there. My parents wouldn't let Claire and me go, though we wanted to. But my friend Lizzie went and she'd told me all about it and I'd been so mad to miss out on it. I'd asked Lizzie if the girl cried. She said no but that a lot of other people did. She said the girl hadn't even peeped and Lizzie thought she was dead, but she wasn't.

A bunch of kids, and adults, too, had jumped the Nail before that, but nobody since. Not that I knew of. The scare had lasted. Somebody had added the girl's name and the date to the roster of names scratched into the sign at the top of the cliff—the sign that said Danger Submerged Rocks No Diving or Jumping. I couldn't remember what her name was, though. And now Diane said Scooter Navarro was going to jump today. Why? I just bet everyone would be there. Maybe even Mike and me.

I didn't feel much like running any farther so I called to Rusty and then turned toward home. What would happen if Mike wanted to go and I said I didn't? Not that Scooter would get hurt or die, probably. There were all kinds of names and dates on that board from successful jumps. Well, maybe not that many. Eight? Nine? There were two marines from Camp Pendleton, and two girls, Karen someone and the other, the one who'd misjudged. Lizzie said she was still at Rancho Los Amigos, living in a wheelchair. Scooter probably wouldn't jump in the end. Maybe Elisa would talk him out of it. Elisa is one of my best friends, but I've hardly seen her since she and Scooter became such a hot twosome. But probably Elisa couldn't stop him, either. Not if he had his mind set on it.

A guy and a girl were laying out towels on the sand as Rusty and I jogged past. The beach day had started. I wished Mike and I were coming down here to lie side by side in the sun, his arm or leg sometimes brushing mine. He'd sit up and look down at me and say, "Hi, Dru!" in that laughing soft way that made me tremble inside. The way I'd trembled that night up at Murchisons. I pounded hard up the steps from the beach, out of breath, knowing it was the memory of that night that had taken my breath away. Already the steps burned under my feet.

"Going to be hot," old Harry Christiansen called to me from the shade of his porch.

"Hot already," I puffed.

It was ten minutes to eight when I ran into our kitchen. The phone was ringing. Mom grabbed it. She held the coffeepot in her other hand.

"Connie Driscoll," she chirped. My mother is a believer in sounding alert and ready for business on the phone, because it could be someone with a million-dollar house to sell. You never know about these things. She looked chirpy, too, in her silky pink robe, her hair brushed back, even a little early lipstick in place.

"Mike!" she said. "Good morning!" She waved the coffeepot happily in my direction. "She just this minute came in. You timed it perfectly. Honey," she said, "it's Mike for you."

I wondered if there was any way to stop a mother from sounding so eager. It truly was her everyday, top-of-the-morning voice, with perhaps just a little extra enthusiasm for Mike. But if I were a guy dating a daughter, that too-cheerful voice would put me off. I hoped it didn't.

I took the phone. "Hi, Mike."

"Hi, yourself. Didn't I see you and your faithful hound on the beach?"

"You did." I signaled to Mom to fill up Rusty's water bowl. He was panting and his tongue dragged on the floor.

"Energetic girl. I'm still in bed." I heard him yawn and tried not to let my imagination become too vivid.

"Want to go to the Nail after lunch and see Scooter Navarro jump?" he asked.

"I heard he was going to," I said.

Rusty slopped water on the linoleum and stepped in the puddle. The bottoms of his ears were wet.

"It's going to be La Paloma's big event," Mike said. "Do you want to go?"

"I'm not sure. Yes and no."

"We don't have to, you know. But I don't think there's any need to be scared. Navarro probably has everything figured out. It's just his ultimate show-off trick."

I ran my finger along a crack in the wall, thin as a spider's web. "Are you going?"

"Maybe. But if you—"

"You want to go, don't you?" I asked.

Mike sounded a bit embarrassed. "Yeah, I guess

I do. It's going to be something to see. But I don't have to . . . there's—"

I interrupted. "No, I'll come with you."

"You will? You're sure?"

"I'm sure."

"Great, then. Scoot says he'll jump at three on the dot, so how's about if I pick you up at two?"

"I'll be ready."

"Date with Mike?" Mom asked as I hung up. I'd never seen her look happier.

I nodded. Maybe if I told her where we were going she'd stop me the way she did when I was in third grade. But I wasn't in third grade anymore, and she wouldn't want to stop me, anyway. Not when I was going with Mike, the future master of El Nido.

TWO

MIKE PARKED HIS CAR on the grassy patch at the head of the Nail. Thistles and wildflowers and bright patches of blowing mustard sometimes brighten the grass, but this close to the edge everything is tufted and stunted.

We got out. Even today a wind gusted and I thought I could taste salt spray on my lips, though that couldn't be. The sea was too far below. Way too far.

A few other cars had been left at the top. Somebody's old red Mustang, the seat and floor littered with burger wrappers and potato-chip bags. Beside it was Laura Jackson's dusty white pickup.

"Not too big an audience," I said. "Maybe Scooter called off the jump."

"Most everybody will drive in below," Mike said. "You can go in as far as Mandela's rock, but there's probably a traffic jam. From here we'll have to walk down the cliff path. I want to get close to the edge and look over—you want to wait here, Dru?"

"Okay." I pushed back my hair and stared at the edge of the Nail. There was nothing beyond it but emptiness and sky.

"Be careful, Mike," I called as he started walking toward the edge. "Don't get too close."

"I won't, don't worry." The wind lifted his thick blond hair, ballooned his yellow-and-white-striped shirt around him, and suddenly I was away after him, putting my hand in his.

"I think I want to look, too."

"Sure?" he asked.

"Sure." We moved slowly forward. Now I could see part of the Deep below, the part farthest from the stem of the Nail. The water was a dark, heaving green, surging around the smoothness of the rocks. If there was spray, I couldn't see it. I clung to Mike's arm as we took another step. Now I saw people on the rocks to the side, blurs of color, the pale ovals of a few faces turned up toward us. Arms waved. I thought I saw Lizzie in her bright red shorts and T-shirt but I wasn't sure. Below us a gull flew, its wings stretched tight like a fan. How strange to be above it. Six feet down from the top of the Nail was the ugly bulge that had to be cleared if you jumped. I wondered about the girl, the one who was in Rancho Los Amigos now in the wheelchair. Maybe she'd smashed into the bulge first, before she fell, tumbling over and over to the rocks below.

"Mike! Mike, please. I can't stand it."

We backed away. I took his other arm and turned to face him. "Do you really think Scooter will do it? Nobody could be that crazy."

Mike jabbed the base of the Danger sign with the toe of his sneaker. "These guys were," he said, and he read off the names scratched into the wood. "Bill Robins. James Robins."

"And look—Myra Constantine. She must be the one who got hurt," I whispered. Myra Constantine, paralyzed forever.

Mike's finger traced a line of carved-out words. "How about this one? 'I jumped and lived.' And here—'I jumped and died.' " He gave me a little nudge and wiggled his fingers in front of my eyes. "Ghosties, coming back in the dead of the night to add their names to the list of fame. The girl in the car . . ."

I slapped at his hand. "Stop it, will you? It's bad enough."

Mike gave me a quick, hard hug. "Sorry, Dru. I couldn't resist."

"I just don't understand why anybody would want to," I mumbled.

Mike shrugged. "Scooter probably just wants to be able to brag. You know how he is. He'll put his name up here and think he's immortal or something."

"Well, why are we going to watch, Mike?"

"Because. . . ," Mike began and stopped.

A blue Chevrolet was rattling across the grass, stopping beside us. Tweeny Chalmers stuck her head out of the open passenger window. "Hi, you two. Is Scooter here yet?"

"Not that we've seen," Mike said. "It's way too early."

Betsy Patterson got out from the driver's side. Betsy and Tweeny are always together. "Are you guys going to watch from up here or are you going down below? Tweeny and I can't decide."

Betsy struggled to put on her red La Paloma windbreaker but a sudden blast of wind whipped it from her and wrapped it around the Danger sign. She grabbed it and rolled it into a ball.

"We're going down, right?" Mike asked me.

"I guess," I said.

Tweeny nodded. "I think we should, too, Betts. There'll be a better view. I mean, what's up here? One second and Scooter will be over the edge. We won't see him hit the water."

Betsy shrugged. "I think it would be more interesting up here. We'd see for ourselves how long it takes him to get up his nerve. How scared he is and all that."

"Oh, for heaven's sake," I said.

The way Betsy's always analyzing people is revolting. She's going to UCLA in the fall to major in psychology, and I guess after that she'll be more revolting than ever.

"But it would be funner to see him in the *air*." Tweeny spread her arms. "Like flying. I wonder what it feels like?"

"He's jumping," Betsy said impatiently, "feet first." She checked her watch. "Oh, well, plenty of time."

The wind had died down. What if it gusted just as Scooter jumped?

"Maybe we should wait up here till he comes and try to talk him out of it. If we all tell him what a stupid risk . . ." I stopped, feeling helpless.

"I doubt if we could talk him out of it, Dru," Mike said gently. "He wouldn't have the nerve not to go through with it. Not now, when everybody knows."

"There's a rumor." Betsy was looking at Mike.

"I don't think it's just a rumor. I think it's true." That was Tweeny, breathless and excited.

I looked from one of them to the other. "What rumor?"

"We haven't heard any rumor," Mike said.

Betsy nodded. "There is one. That Elisa might be going to jump with him."

My stomach lurched. "Elisa? No! She wouldn't be so stupid."

"Yes, she would." Betsy sounded irritated, as if *I* were the stupid one. "I heard it was some kind of pact. To show how much they love each other or something."

"But that's . . . that's ridiculous." I could feel tears pushing at the back of my eyes. Bad enough that Scooter Navarro was going to do this. But Elisa! Scooter was part of the in crowd in school and I hardly knew him. It was the crowd of rich kids in their torn designer jeans, or the jocks in their letterman jackets, or the cheerleaders like Diane and Tweeny and Betsy, or the special ones like Mike who were new and smart and gorgeous, or the dangerous ones like Scooter and Hopi and their friends. With Scooter, Elisa had become part of the in crowd. How odd that I'd ended up being part of it, too, because of Mike.

Lizzie had explained it to me when I'd wondered how it happened. "It's like in the movies when the working girl marries the big boss. It's that simple. In politics they'd say you rode in on his coattails." Lizzie is smart. In fall she's going to be working part-time for IBM and they're paying her college tuition.

"Mike's coattails aren't that bad," I had said and Lizzie'd grinned.

"I'd say he has the best coattails in town."

"If Elisa wants to show Scooter she loves him, she should stop him," I told Betsy now.

Betsy gave me one of her I-know-the-human-soul-and-you-don't looks. "It doesn't work that way, Dru. Sharing danger with a loved one has always been a way of bonding, all the way from pagan times. Lovers' leaps. Suicide pacts. They happen."

I turned to Mike. "She doesn't mean this is a *suicide* pact?"

"No, of course not. This is another one of Scooter's stunts. It's just bigger, that's all." Mike wiped the corners of my eyes with his thumbs.

"What's with the tears?" He didn't know what I knew about Elisa. Not too many people did. She'd told Lizzie, too, of course. But we'd promised Elisa never to tell anyone else. "I guess that's the way she wants it," I'd said, and Lizzie had nodded.

"It's just the wind," I explained now, and I tried to put the awful rumor about Elisa out of my head.

"Yeah, the wind." He hugged me hard. This was Mike Moriarty hugging me in front of Betsy and Tweeny and God and everyone. Sam Moriarty's son. My mother would have been ecstatic.

"Would you like to go home, Dru?" Mike was asking me, his eyes soft and loving. "We don't have to stay."

"Go home?" Betsy shrieked. "That's not fair. If they're going to do it, the least we can do is be supportive. If a tree falls in the forest and there's no one to hear, does it really count?"

Mike held his hands in front of his face as if to protect himself. "Oh, Betsy, give us a break, will you?"

I looked at Mike. "I wish I'd known about Elisa. I might have been able to talk her out of it. I'm still going to try. She used to listen to me. Maybe I should try to get Lizzie up here, too."

And then we heard the *putt-putt* of the small red

motor scooter coming across the grass. We all know that red machine. Scooter tootles about on it all the time. That's how he got his name. He rode it to school every day. Once he made a ramp out of a barrel and a plank of wood and rode the scooter up it, flying over the other side. Somebody said he'd jumped the gap between the flat roofs of Chile Coastburgers and Rick's Surf Shop. But that didn't seem possible.

"You don't think he's going to go over the Nail on the scooter?" Tweeny squeaked. "Man, that would be crazy."

"No way," Betsy muttered. "If he did, his precious bike would be gone forever."

I shaded my eyes. I could see Elisa on the little seat behind Scooter. They were both wearing black wet suits.

"They *are* both going to jump," I whispered. "They are."

THREE

SCOOTER AND ELISA wore helmets, which I thought was pretty ironic. They were going to jump the Nail, and yet they were being careful in traffic. Unless they planned to jump with their helmets on . . . If you hit the rocks, then a helmet might help. But wouldn't the weight of a helmet pull you down when you hit the water, down into that terrible darkness? I clenched my jaws.

"Hi!" Scooter's smile was wide and carefree. "Here for the action?"

He didn't seem nervous at all, but he had to be. Had he come up here earlier, looked over that cliff, stood right on the edge where, if you leaned forward, you could see the bulge? Had he thought how it would be to throw himself forward into nothingness? And what was Elisa thinking?

Scooter unfastened the strap of his helmet, then held out a hand to Elisa, who still sat on the bike, her feet in the grass on either side. They both had on short surfing boots. Elisa swung herself off the bike and Scooter pulled down the kickstand.

"Hi." Elisa included all of us in her wavering smile, but she didn't look at me directly. Her gaze drifted beyond us to the edge of the Nail, then back to Scooter. He was taking something from the small box strapped on the back of the bike. It was a screwdriver with a green wooden handle.

"Let's see now . . ." He walked across to the Danger sign while we watched him, the five of us standing in a line like birds on a wire. "What do you think, babe?" he asked Elisa. "Should we put our names on the end of the list here or start a new column of our own?"

"I don't care." Elisa took off her helmet and her straight hair tumbled down, red as fire. Elisa has the most beautiful hair. That's even what it says under her picture in the La Paloma yearbook, *the girl with the most beautiful hair*. A whip of wind lifted it, blew it in a red mane behind her. The wind whistled through a gap at the top of the sign, found a loose chrome strip on Laura Jackson's truck and rattled it like someone beating on a metal drum.

I couldn't seem to swallow.

"You know what? Let's start our own list, babe."

The wind made a white center part in Scooter's thick black curls. "Then if anyone else cares to try, after we've broken ground—" He stopped. "I should say broken *water* but that sounds kind of gross . . . anyway, they can put their names after ours."

"Okay." Elisa's whisper was so soft I could hardly hear it. She cleared her throat. "Okay."

I held out a hand to her. "Elisa . . ."

"Don't," she said. "Don't, Dru."

Scooter began to scratch a big S into the wood with the blade of the screwdriver. Betsy took a step toward him. "Hey, now. Wait just a second. It's not fair putting your name on there before you do it. After all, you might—" She stopped.

Scooter paused in the act of gouging the S deeper in the wood. "We might what, Betsy? Be dead? Be crippled? So what? We'll still have jumped, won't we? It'll still count."

"I wasn't going to say that." Betsy put her hands on her hips. "I meant, you might decide *not* to jump and then your names would be on the board and it wouldn't be true."

Scooter gave her a wide-eyed look. "Don't sweat it. We'll jump."

Mike let go of my hand and went across to the

sign. "It's really windy, Scooter. Maybe you should call it off for now and try another day."

"It's always windy up here at the Nail, so what's the diff?" He'd started on the *C* now, and somehow the rest of us had moved in closer to watch.

"I'm glad we stayed up here," Tweeny whispered to me. "The guys down below are missing all this part. I guess this is why the Scoot came early . . . you know, to get their names up. Afterward they'll probably want to go straight home."

I closed my eyes. How could Betsy listen to Tweeny's prattle? Maybe when she got to be a real psychologist she'd figure out why she and Tweeny were best friends.

Scooter glanced at Elisa. "How're you doin', babe?"

"I need to go to the bathroom," Elisa said. She turned to me. "Is there a bathroom someplace?"

I shook my head. "Not up here. I don't think there's one down below, either. You'd have to go all the way to the beach."

Scooter grinned. "Hold on till we hit the water, babe, then let go. Nobody'll know. Believe me, nobody'll care."

"Look, can I talk to you a minute?" I asked Elisa.

She looked at Scooter, and I stepped forward so I was between them. "Just you," I urged.

"Sure, go ahead," Scooter said. "Just don't go trying to talk her out of it, Dru. You couldn't anyway."

How cocky he was! I moved to where we couldn't be heard, and after another quick glance at Scooter, Elisa followed me.

"You don't have to jump just because he's going to," I told her. "You're a separate person. You can decide for yourself."

Elisa shivered. "Sometimes a person has to go along. There are things to prove."

"What things? Nothing that's worth this. You could *die*, Elisa." I was looking directly into her eyes, gripping her arms in their cold black sheaths. The wind had stopped now and I could hear the faint *scratch, scratch* of the screwdriver on wood. Music drifted from somewhere below.

"When was the last time you saw Doctor Manriquez?" I let go of her arms.

Elisa shrugged. "I stopped going."

"Did you stop taking your pills, too? Tell me, Elisa."

"I don't need them anymore. I don't feel—you know . . ."

"Depressed," I finished.

"Scooter made things okay for me," Elisa said angrily.

"Oh, sure." I took her arms again. "Don't do it, Elisa," I said. "Please don't."

"I have to," Elisa said and pushed past me to stand again with Scooter. "How's it going, babe?" she asked him.

He turned his wrist so he could see the face of the diving watch he wore. "Man, I didn't know getting our names on here would be such a drag. This is *slow!* Only fifteen minutes till we're set to jump, and we don't want to keep our public waiting. Hey, Mike! Catch!"

He swung his arm and the green-handled screwdriver came twirling like a baton through the air. Mike caught it.

"Finish our names, will you? And don't forget to put in the date, buddy, and bracket me and Elisa together. A little heart would be nice." He drew one with a finger in the air.

"Are you really going through with this, Scoot?" I asked.

He mimicked my wavery voice. "Yes, Dru. We really are."

I couldn't believe this guy. Was he really so cool, so casual?

He spoke again to Mike then, sounding as if this

were just another ordinary day. "Do something else for me, Mikey. You and Dru are going down on the rocks, right?"

Mike nodded.

"Take my bike down with you, okay? When Elisa and I get out of the water we'll want our transportation waiting. In fact, why don't you and Dru ride it down? The keys are in it. You'll have to come up afterward to get your car anyway so you can finish recording our names for posterity then."

I remembered Mike saying, "He thinks it'll make him immortal." That's what he wanted to be—immortal.

Mike ran his hands through his hair. "Scooter? Give it up. It's not worth—"

"See you down there, man. Take off now, you and Dru, or you'll miss the show. Elisa and I, we're taking the short route."

"Come on, Dru." Mike took hold of my hand.

Behind us I heard Tweeny ask, "What about us, Betsy? We should go down now, too."

Betsy answered, "Sh! Wait a few more minutes, okay?" I could tell Betsy was squirreling away psychology tidbits so she could munch on them for the next month.

Was there any point in arguing with Elisa again?

I looked back at her pale face, at the red hair drifting around her. As if she'd read my mind she shook her head.

"Hey." Scooter's voice made us pause. "Put your helmets on, you two." He thumped the top of the sign. "Accidents can happen, you know, fast as this."

"He's crazy," I whispered, "really, truly crazy. Somebody ought to lock him up."

I waited till Mike got the scooter started before I got on behind him. It was such a small machine, like a kid's toy. You'd think someone like Scooter would have a flashy Harley. But he liked to do the unexpected thing. He got a kick out of surprising people.

"See you later, kids," he yelled.

I held on tight as Mike and I rattled over the field. At the turn to the highway I looked back. They were all so small, standing there, the sky big and empty and endless behind them. We turned onto the road and I couldn't see them anymore.

FOUR

MIKE HAD BEEN right about the traffic on the dirt road below. Cars and trucks were pulled in nose to tail all the way to Mandela's rock. Last one in would have to be first one out. Mike maneuvered the scooter through the small gaps and onto the footpath that led close to the brink of the Deep. There were some regular bikes propped this far in. A few kids must have cycled the seven miles from town.

Rock music blasted from a radio somewhere. I looked around. There were maybe twenty or thirty people here. I recognized most of them from school, but a few were strangers our age or younger. The news had spread from town to town. That underground teen network had done a good job.

Hopi was the first to see us. Hopi has long straight black hair that he holds back with a red bandanna on his forehead, and he wears fringed moccasin boots. He tells people that his grandfather was the son of a Hopi Indian chief, which may be true. I have no idea. His real name is Fred Gowland, and although he and Scooter are friends, Hopi's the closest thing Scooter has to a rival. They both get a charge out of danger.

Mike cut the little *putt-putt* of the motor, and Hopi came pushing through the crowd that had surrounded us. "What are you two doing on Scooter's bike? I guess you just brought it down for him. And is his friend, female gender, jumping, too?" He grinned widely.

"She is," Mike said, unsmiling.

Lizzie sat on a flat rock close to the water's edge making signs for us to come over.

Diane was waving, too. She was sitting with the McInerney twins, Tom and Grant, laughing, punching Tom's arm. What a fun summer afternoon!

Mike and I hung the helmets on the handlebars, and Mike locked the bike, which seemed pretty pointless to me. Everybody knows that scooter. Stealing it would be like trying to steal the Jewel of the Nile. He put the keys in the pocket of his shorts, where I could see the green handle of the screwdriver sticking up.

Jeremy Poulson was standing right next to me.

Jeremy and I know each other pretty well. We did an English project together once.

"I called the Scoot last night when I got home from work," he whispered.

"You did?"

I turned to look at Mike, but he had moved to another rock to talk to someone and wasn't listening.

"I told Scooter my mom's a volunteer at Rancho Los Amigos. She goes every Saturday. I told him about the girl, you know, the one who jumped that time and hit the rocks." Jeremy swallowed. "My mom says she can move her arms, and feed herself, and get around in her wheelchair, but she can't even sit on her own. They have to prop her up some way. And she'll never walk . . ." He stopped. "Course, as Scooter says, she's the only one we know about that jumped and had something bad happen."

"Yeah," I said. "But one out of how many? There aren't exactly a bunch of names up on the board." I looked around. It was like party time down here, like a big picnic. I even saw a bucket of the Colonel's chicken. A couple of candy wrappers and a Pepsi can floated on the dark surface of the Deep. So much for the environment, I thought.

Talk about it, but don't bother to take your garbage home. I was wishing I hadn't glanced at the Deep, though. There was something so frightening about that still blackness. Easy to believe there was no bottom here, that the hole went through to the center of the earth. There was no lightening of the dark, no sparkle of sun on water. The cliff would keep the Deep always in shadow. I looked at the stem of the Nail, where the cliff disappeared below the surface of the water. I let my gaze move up over the clumps of weeds growing out of the black pocked rock, over a cluster of loose gravel where the stone had eroded, over the swelling of the bulge to the head of the Nail itself. It was like a diving platform—but higher than any diving platform would ever be.

Mike returned and tapped my shoulder. "Did you see the guys in the boat?" He pointed to where a small motorboat buzzed in narrow circles in the sea beyond the opening to the Deep.

"They *were* anchored," Jeremy said. "But they were bobbing up and down, and then Hopi and a couple of his friends tried to swim out to them and they started circling again. They spotted Diane and one of them began yelling at her."

"What do you mean, yelling at her?" I asked.

"Oh, yelling, 'Hey, Blondie! You in the white shorts. Why don't *you* swim out?' Stuff like that."

I didn't look at Mike. Diane was definitely spottable. I shouldn't have asked.

Mike shaded his eyes. "Where did they come from?"

Jeremy shrugged. "Who knows? Probably some guys just fishing till they saw the crowds."

Lizzie was shouting my name now and waving us over.

"Do you want to come and sit with us?" I asked Jeremy.

He shook his head. "I don't think I could sit. I don't even know if I'll be able to watch. I think I came because I'm still hoping they won't—"

The crowd whistled and clapped.

Scooter and Elisa stood on the edge holding hands. Scooter waved. I could see that Elisa was at least a step behind him.

"This is it," Mike said grimly.

"I hope they've made their wills," Jeremy added.

But this wasn't it.

Scooter and Elisa disappeared again, and around us on the rocks there was a sigh, like wind moving. Somebody pitched a rolled-up Fritos bag at the cliff. It fell beside the candy wrappers.

"Do you think they've changed their minds?" I asked Mike. "Jeremy called Scooter last night."

"Not because of that they didn't," Jeremy said.

In the crowd someone began a chant: "Jump! Jump! Jump!" and "Nail it! Nail it!"

And then there was another burst of cheering. I looked up at the Nail again, my heart pounding, but this time the encouragement wasn't for Scooter and Elisa. Betsy and Tweeny were shuffling down the cliff path, Betsy in front, Tweeny with one hand on Betsy's shoulder.

"Betsy, Tweeny, Betsy, Tweeny," the crowd chanted. I sensed their relief that something was happening. That anything was happening. Betsy slipped and slid onto her bottom, grabbed a clump of weeds, and was up again. The cheering got louder.

"We have to go sit with Lizzie," I told Jeremy. "See you later."

Mike and I began to pick our way through legs, jumping rock to rock. The water must come up this far during storms or maybe it's the sea fog that makes the rocks mossy and slippery. A tiny crab no bigger than a dime raced into a crack in front of us. Now we were in the shadow of the Nail ourselves, and the air seemed dank, as if we were underground.

Lizzie had spread a Mickey Mouse towel on the rock. "Hi," she said. "I just heard about Elisa when I got down here. Did you talk to her, Dru? She's not going to go through with it, is she? I know Scooter will, but—"

"She is," I said. "Oh, Lizzie! What if . . ." I couldn't finish the sentence or the thought. "I wish I wasn't here. But maybe, you know, she might need someone."

"I couldn't bear to miss it," Lizzie said. "Why is that? I must be some kind of a monster. But I didn't know about Elisa. This could set her back."

"She's quit her pills," I whispered.

We stared at each other.

Mike had snuggled down behind me, one leg stretched out on either side of me, his arms around my waist. I could see the blond fuzz on those brown arms and legs, the little goose bumps that had come with the cold. More than anything I wanted to turn and bury my face against him, and cry, and have him comfort me. I wanted him to stroke my hair and tell me Elisa was going to be all right. But we were still too new with each other. A tiny spider raced across his knee. I picked it off, feeling for a second the cool roughness of his skin. "Spider," I told him over my shoulder and felt my face flush.

Suddenly his arms were tighter around my waist.

"Lizzie," I whispered, and all three of us stared up at the Nail. It was empty. But everyone was looking up. Why? Why was there suddenly this awful stillness? Who had said? Who knew? How did we all know?

There was no sound as Elisa and Scooter came flying off the cliff.

It wasn't the way I'd imagined it would be, but in that first, heart-stopping second I realized it was the only way it could be—if they weren't to hit the bulge.

The two of them must have paced back, about as far as the wind-battered Danger sign. They'd probably stood there for a second or two, saying things to each other. Scooter would say, "Remember what I told you, babe. Do what I do."

"I'm scared, Scooter, so scared."

"Trust me, babe. There's nothing to it."

They would have run then at full speed, holding hands, jumped, their momentum carrying them out and over the bulge.

They looked so small, dropping through the air, Elisa's hair streaming red above her head.

A flock of gulls nesting on the rocky ledges flew off, their shrieks mingling with the two splashes as Scooter and Elisa hit the water and disappeared.

I didn't know how long it had taken from top to

bottom. Four seconds? Five? I only knew that they'd missed the rocks. Thank God, they'd missed the rocks. We were all scrambling up, crowding as close to the Deep as we could get, peering down into the water. There was some scattered applause but it never got going.

Where *were* they? Why hadn't they surfaced? How far down . . . ?

Lizzie was clutching my arm, her nails digging into me. Mike's arms were still around my waist, though we were all three standing. "Where—?" I began.

And then there was no more silence, only cheering, as first Scooter and then Elisa bobbed to the surface.

I couldn't take my eyes off Elisa, her face sickly pale, her hair plastered dark and dripping against her skull. She gulped for air, gasping as she paddled water.

"Are you okay, babe?" Scooter called to her, and she said, "Okay," the word coming between two hiccups or sobs. Scooter swam over, put one arm around her, and began paddling toward the rocks. His head was a mass of wet corkscrew ringlets, and he was laughing.

"Wow!" he yelled. "What a blast!"

Arms reached for them, but nobody was close enough.

Scooter grabbed the rocks. His hands slipped off the green slime, and the surge of the water pulled him and Elisa back again.

Hopi knotted two towels together, lay on his stomach, wound one end around his wrist, and tossed the other to Scooter.

"Thanks, buddy," Scooter said as Hopi reeled him in.

He was out now, his boots sliding, kneeling to help Elisa. She clambered up, retching, holding on to him. One of her feet was bare.

Scooter pulled a streamer of seaweed out of her hair. I'd never seen him look at her so tenderly, so lovingly. "You did fine, babe. Just fine," he told her.

I jumped the rocks to where they stood and took both her cold hands in mine. "Elisa."

She looked at me blankly.

"Elisa, it's Dru. You're safe. It's over."

"I've got her," Scooter said and put his arm around her shoulders.

The crowd made way for them to get through, Elisa drooping, head bent, her one bare foot red and mottled.

"How was it, Scooter?" someone asked. I think it might have been Jill Ebsco, who plays in the school band.

Scooter smiled. "Awesome."

"See any octopi?" That was one of the twins.

"Not a one. But there was a shark humongous enough to take your head off in one bite, McInerney." Scooter couldn't seem to stop grinning.

"Where's the bike?" he asked, and Mike pointed while several other helpful voices called, "Over there. On the path, Scoot."

"I locked it. Here are the keys," Mike said.

"Thanks." Scooter tossed them hand to hand. "I'll take the screwdriver, too. Got a job I have to finish." Scooter raised his voice. "I've decided Elisa and I are going up to the Nail to record this ourselves for posterity. Why don't you all come watch? It's history in the making, guys."

"Wait a sec," I said. "Elisa's frozen solid. She's got to go home, Scooter. Why doesn't somebody else drive her? Tom? That's your car right at the end. You could take Elisa, couldn't you?"

Scooter shook his head. "Wait up! My lady and I came together and we'll leave together."

"Well, Tom could take you both. Mike and I'll bring the scooter and . . ."

Elisa hadn't yet lifted her head.

"I'll tell you what," Scooter said. "You go ahead and do it, Mike. The rest of you guys go with him, see he gets it right. I'll take my lady home."

I tried one more time. "Elisa? Elisa? Wouldn't you be warmer in a car?"

She didn't answer.

"Gimme the keys and I'll unlock the bike for you," Hopi offered, and Scooter handed them over as if he was conferring some great honor. Water dripped down his and Elisa's wet suits, darkening the dirt path.

Hopi turned the bike in the right direction and Scooter got on.

"Give Elisa a hand, will you, Hopi?" he asked, and Hopi made a big thing out of getting Elisa into the seat behind.

"We'll have you home in no time flat," Scooter told her in that same loving voice. "And Mike, my man! I'll be back to inspect your work."

He looked around at the rest of us. "Well," he asked. "Who's next?"

"Who's next what?" I asked Lizzie.

"I think he means to jump," Lizzie said grimly.

Scooter shook water from his black curls and looked over his shoulder at the Nail. "I'll tell you something. That baby up there, that's what separates the men from the boys." He stretched a hand back and patted Elisa's leg. "And the women from the girls, right, babe?"

The scooter purred into life as he turned the key. "So who's next?"

We all stood watching them go, then someone yelled, "Hey, look!"

Elisa's little black boot had surfaced and was floating, shredded and torn, on the top of the water.

FIVE

THE MCINERNEY TWINS' car was the last one parked on the path to the Deep. Grant said they'd give us a ride to the top of the Nail to get Mike's car. Diane came, too, of course, sitting in front on Tom's lap, while Mike and I got in back.

The rest of the cars followed us out.

I was shivering, and Mike put his arm loosely around my shoulders. Diane watched us in the rearview mirror.

"Well," she said. "Scooter and Elisa gave some performance! Didn't she look awful?"

"Wouldn't you?" I asked and thought, probably not. You'd probably pop up from the Deep smiling that million-dollar smile, every blond hair glistening.

"Well," Grant said to his twin. "I guess we won our bet."

"What bet was that?" Mike asked.

"We bet that Elisa would jump, too," Tom said.

"A bunch of the guys thought she wouldn't when it came right to it. But we knew she would. She'd do anything for Scooter."

Grant gave a snort of a laugh. "Nice for Scooter."

We were on the highway now, and I stared blankly at the traffic coming in the other direction, heading for town or shopping or the beach. There were businessmen in suits and ties, kids our age with surfboards strapped on their roof racks—out-of-towners, probably, who'd get hassled in the water by the locals for stealing our waves. I thought how lucky they were not to know what had happened, maybe not even to know the Nail was there.

"She'd do anything for Scooter," Tom had scoffed, and I remembered Elisa telling me, "There are things to prove." What things? That she loved him? Was that something you had to prove?

"Hey!" Diane turned to smile at Mike. "Did you see that car with the SDSU sticker? You'll have to get yourself one of those."

"San Diego State University," Grant said to Tom and rolled his eyes. "An okay football team, but overrated. Not like Penn."

"Do you think you'll have Friday classes, Mike?" Diane asked.

"I don't know yet. I'll only be going part-time."

She smiled. "Well, let's both try for Fridays. Then I could bum a ride home with you some weekends. Okay?"

"Sure," Mike said.

I looked out of the window again. We had turned into the meadow that ends abruptly at the edge of the Nail. The wheels of the car crunched over the little clumps of wild mustard that grew close to the road. Probably Diane and Mike would see each other a lot. I imagined them running into each another in the cafeteria or the student union . . . driving back to La Paloma together along Coast Highway, the moon on the water, music playing on Mike's radio. My eyes met Tom's in the rearview mirror and I knew his thoughts weren't too happy, either. Wasn't there a whiny country-and-western song about old flames and how quickly they could start up again?

A gust of wind buffeted the car and brought my thoughts back to Elisa.

Grant pulled on the wheel. "Feel that? If I were a superstitious guy I'd think something was telling us to stay away from here."

"Too late now," I said, noticing that the white pickup truck and Betsy's car were still parked.

Grant stopped as close to the Danger sign as he

could get. The wind snatched the door the second Mike opened it, swinging it back hard on its hinges. He grabbed my arm so I wouldn't get blown away. "I don't want to stay!" I shouted against the wind. "Let's ask someone else to put their names up. I want to stop on the way home so I can check up on Elisa." Just as I said the last word the wind died, leaving the five of us standing in silence, the name Elisa sliding past us, dissolving in space.

"What's this about Elisa?" Diane asked. She was holding on to the blue-and-white-checked jockey cap that exactly matched her checked shirt.

"Elisa?" I said. "I was just thinking about her, that's all."

"She's okay." Diane leaned forward to examine the sign. "She's probably feeling great, as a matter of fact. How many girls' names do you see up here?"

"There are two," Grant said. "The girl who got hurt and Karen somebody. Didn't you see it? It says, 'I jumped inside my head, and died.' "

"Smart girl to just do it inside her head," Mike said.

Diane made a face. "Still, Elisa must think she's pretty unique."

Hadn't Diane noticed how destroyed Elisa had been? Who cared about unique?

It seemed as if everybody was arriving now. There was a lot of car-door banging and laughing and calling back and forth about how incredible the jump had been. I saw Hopi and his group of friends in their trademark black sweatshirts. Hopi had taken his off and tied the sleeves around his waist. His chest was bare, smooth and golden brown. A snake tattoo crept up one of his arms. He'd told us once that snakes were sacred to the Hopis and that even now there are festivals in Arizona where Hopis carry rattlesnakes in their mouths in a ceremonial dance.

"Yeah, but they take the fangs out first," Scooter had said.

"No way. What good is a rattlesnake without fangs? You might as well be dancing with a bunny rabbit. No danger, no thrill, Scoot."

Scooter had laughed. "I should have been an Indian, you know it? Sometime I'd like to go dancing with you and those snakes, Hopi." And then the two of them had clasped hands in the power shake. Two of a kind, all right.

Hopi was twirling something in his fingers now, and I saw that it was Elisa's boot. He must have fished it out of the Deep. "Pretty chewed up," he said in his slow, deep drawl. "Maybe the Scoot wasn't kidding when he said there was a shark down there." He tossed the boot to me. "You want to hold on to it for her?"

It was cold and slippery and still damp.

"Let's see it, Dru." That was Lizzie. She touched Elisa's boot. "Ugh!" Lizzie said. "Slime time."

Mike took the screwdriver from the pocket of his shorts. "We've got to go. Would somebody . . . ?"

"Give it here," Hopi said.

Mike slapped the green handle into his hand and Hopi twirled the screwdriver, the movement making the snake tattoo wriggle. He went to the sign, examined it, and began working where Scooter had stopped. The wind gusted again, flaring his long hair, flapping the fringe on the tops of his moccasins. He blew on the wood, clearing the paint chips, and started to carve the *O*.

"Do we have to stay any longer?" I whispered to Mike.

"No," he said. "We don't."

"You're not leaving, are you?" Betsy asked. "This is history, guys. Maybe we'll never see another name go up on this board."

"Oh yes, you will." Hopi ran his fingers over Scooter's half-finished name on the sign and began on the second *O*. "Didn't you hear the Scoot ask who's jumping next? Well, you're looking at him."

"You mean—*you?*" Lizzie asked.

"Don't, Hopi." I turned Elisa's boot in my hand. "Just *don't*."

"Tomorrow?" Tweeny squeaked. "Or now? We could all go back down. You should do it now while we're hot."

Hopi tossed his hair over one shoulder and gave us a narrow-eyed look. "Naw. Today belongs to Scooter. And ritual's important. Scooter started it and I'll keep it going. Same day, same time, next week. After that, who knows? The summer's just beginning."

"Don't be stupid," Mike said. "Just because Scooter and Elisa made it doesn't mean—"

Betsy interrupted. "Will you jump alone, Hopi? It's psychologically recognized that a danger shared—"

Hopi didn't let her finish. "Are you volunteering, Betsy?" Betsy stepped back.

Hopi grinned. "I didn't think so." He straightened and looked at each of us. "Listen up," he said. But he didn't need to tell us to listen. He had our total attention. "Let's keep today's jump and the next one quiet. Word gets around and some nosy adults will come busting in to stop us. Then the fun will be over."

"We won't say anything," Tweeny said breathlessly. "Honest."

Hopi shook back his hair. "Tell your friends if you want. I like crowds. Next Friday, three o'clock. But don't forget what they used to say, never trust anybody over thirty. Make that over twenty."

"Can you believe this?" Lizzie whispered to me. She had draped her towel over her shoulders and one of Mickey Mouse's dark eyes watched me intently.

I felt sick. "Let's go, Mike," I said. "Now."

Nobody cared that we were leaving. There were other things to think about. Not a single head turned as Mike started the car. I set Elisa's boot on the seat between us and rubbed my fingers on my shirt.

We didn't talk as the car bounced across the grass, then Mike said softly, "Uh-oh! Bad timing."

Scooter had just turned into the meadow from the highway. He stopped when he saw us, one black-booted foot balancing him on the ground. How weird he looked in the round red helmet, his body slick in the tight black wet suit. He could have been an alien from another planet.

"Hopi's getting the names up on the board. He's about halfway done," Mike told him.

"Okay. How come you guys are leaving?"

I leaned across Mike. "We're going home. And I want to see Elisa."

Scooter made the bike motor growl then purr. "That's not a good idea," he said. "She's tired. She's going to take a nap." He spotted the torn boot on the seat. "And you can toss that. It's no good anymore."

"That will be up to Elisa," I said.

Behind us there was a sudden cheer. I turned to look back and saw the crowd, whooping and yelling, waving their arms for Scooter to come. Scooter grinned.

"I better get over there." He made a doughnut wheelie in the grass and roared off.

Mike looked at me. "We're still going to Elisa's?"

"Yes." I sat back.

"You know, we didn't tell Scooter there's going to be a repeat performance of his jump," Mike said.

"They'll tell him soon enough," I said. "One thing for sure, I won't be in the audience next time."

But I was.

Six

WE WERE BOTH QUIET on the way back to La Paloma. I kept remembering Elisa's face, her blank, unseeing eyes. I touched the boot that lay between Mike and me. He covered my hand with his and said, "I know, sweetheart. I know." Then his voice brightened. "Hey—I was going to tell you. Last night my father talked to me about your mom."

I tried to smile. "A hot romance from the past, I guess."

"Really hot. He says she was the cutest girl at La Paloma High. Peppy, he says. Full of life." Mike raised an eyebrow at me and grinned.

Nice Mike, I thought. Trying to distract me.

"She hasn't changed much," I said, picturing my mom the way she is now, dashing in from work or on the phone, sparkling and vivacious. I didn't let myself think of the way she sometimes is, when she seems to be blaming my dad, or life, for not giving her all the things she thinks she should have. "She's peppy still," I said. *"And* pretty."

Mike gave me another sideways glance. "Yeah. Remember? That's what my dad said that night in the restaurant. 'You're as beautiful as ever, Connie.' I didn't hear her telling *him* he was as beautiful as ever. Now what kind of a sexist attitude is that?"

At any other time I'd have been really interested in hearing about my mom and Mike's dad. But now I had too many other things to think about.

I looked at the ocean beyond West Beach, the sailboarders skimming their Windsurfers like butterflies across the water, the last of the sun worshipers gathering up their towels and lotions, drowsy with sun and sea air. Normally I'd have loved driving along here with Mike, being with him so close in his car that I could feel the warmth of his leg next to mine. But today was different. Bad things had happened and I could feel worse things coming.

"Did you know your mom saw your dad for the first time on graduation night in nineteen sixty-five? It was up at the club and she was my father's date."

"I know. She told me."

"I guess your dad was playing the piano and—"

I interrupted. "And she saw him and he saw *her* and that was it. Love at first sight. And three months later they were married."

"And my father was so bummed out he left La Paloma," Mike said. "He went to San Jose to work in Uncle Jack's construction business, wheeling barrows of dirt and laying bricks."

"And now he's back," I said lightly. "An all-American success story." There were things I could have added but didn't. "Here's Elisa's street. Turn left."

Mike was driving slowly. "Man, am I glad my dad and your mom *didn't* end up getting married. You'd have been my sister. I don't think I could have handled that."

I smiled. "Impossible," I said. "There's the house, Mike. Oh, I hope Elisa's okay." I was really tempted to tell him about Elisa's problems, but I'd promised.

"I don't want anybody but you guys to know," she'd told Lizzie and me. "Nobody!" So instead I said, "I have real bad vibes about this, Mike."

I know 64 Atascadero really well. I've been to sleepovers here and come home with Elisa sometimes after school, to snack and talk and dream about what we wanted in our futures. "High fashion model," Elisa always said. "Teacher," I'd say, and she'd push me and shake her head. "Teacher! What a drag!" I was here, too, on a lot of nights when things were bad for Elisa. But it's been a while.

The house looked the same, though, same flaking brown paint, same bamboo blinds lowered on the small windows, the lawn mowed but grass growing in clumps against the walls.

"A fixer-upper," my mom would have called it, and she'd know the price range right away. "Not the best part of town," she'd add, but not the worst, either.

Mike stopped at the curb. "You want me to come in?" he asked. I shook my head. "Well, take your time. I have this." He pulled a Stephen King paperback from the glove compartment and turned on the car radio.

"Thanks." I touched his hand, took my purse and Elisa's boot, and ran up the path to the house. The place looked deserted, but it always does. When I rang the bell it seemed to echo in emptiness. I glanced at my watch. Elisa lives with her mom. Mrs. Fratello waitresses down at the Strand Cafe and has all sorts of hours and shifts. She was probably still at work. And maybe Elisa *was* taking a nap. I tried the door.

"Elisa?" I stepped into the living room. It smelled of coffee and cigarette smoke, her mom's staple diet.

"Elisa?" I called at the bottom of the stairs. "Are you there?"

No answer.

I went quickly up, remembering the squeaks and creaks from nights I'd stayed here, Elisa and Lizzie and me sneaking down after midnight to make popcorn or eat ice cream.

I knocked on her door, waited, opened it. Where could she be if she wasn't here?

She was here. She was sitting on the edge of one of the twin beds, still in the wet suit. Her head was bowed. She was shaking and she felt cold as ice when I touched her.

"Elisa," I said. "Why don't you just stand up for a minute and I'll help get you out of this thing." I had to pull her up so I could unzip the wet suit and peel it off her, pulling each arm out, the way you would with a little kid. I took the comforter from the other bed and wrapped it around her, then went to the bathroom and turned on the shower.

"Come on, Elisa." Arms around her, I eased her into the bathroom and helped her over the edge of the tub. I drew the shower curtain closed.

Through the striped plastic, spotted with colored fish and mildew, I could see her standing motionless, the hot water hissing down on her. After about five minutes I turned the faucets off, helped get her dry, wrapped a towel around her dripping hair, and led her back to her room. There was a big sweatshirt tossed on a chair. I got it onto her, dried her hair as best I could, and bundled her into bed. The other comforter was still in the bathroom, so I went back for it and piled that one on top of her, too.

"Feel better?" I asked. "Warmer?"

She nodded.

"Shall I make you something hot to drink? Tea? Would you like tea?"

She turned her face away.

"Are you sick, Elisa? Should I call your mom?"

"No." The word was so loud it made me jump. "No. I was just cold. I'm okay now."

"You didn't hit your head or—"

"No. Just cold."

"Stay put." I ran downstairs, filled the kettle, and put it on to boil, found a mug and a tea bag that said Sweet Dreams on it and smelled of flowers when I added the water. I carried the mug carefully back upstairs and knelt next to the bed.

"Here." I raised her head on my arm so she could sip.

"Too hot," she began, and then, her head higher, she saw the boot where I'd dropped it on the floor and gave a piercing shriek.

"Wait. Wait. It's nothing." I set the mug on the bedside table and picked up the boot. "See? It's just this. It floated up and Hopi—"

"Oh no. Oh no. Oh no."

She had both hands over her face now.

"Look, Elisa. Don't freak out on me. I'm sorry I brought the thing. Scooter said to toss it. I'll take it downstairs."

"Put it down. Don't touch it." She had scrunched her head as far back into the pillows as it could go.

"All right. Look, I'll drop it. Look. I'll kick it under the bed."

"Is it torn?" Elisa asked in a small shaky voice.

"Yeah. It's no good anymore. I think maybe it got caught—"

"She pulled it off," Elisa said.

"Who?" I lifted her hair and spread its wetness gently across the pillows.

"The drowned girl. The one in the car. Down, down, down . . ."

Elisa was shuddering, the way Rusty does when he's having a bad dream. And that's what she was having. "Sh," I whispered. "Everything's all right."

She moaned. "You don't believe me. I knew you wouldn't. Nobody will. So what's the use?"

"I didn't say I didn't believe you." I lifted the mug of tea again but she pushed it away and some of it spilled onto the comforter.

"The girl caught my foot. She wasn't going to let go."

"Well," I said softly, "she did let go." Talking in my Rusty Dog voice again, the one I use to quiet and soothe him.

"Stop it!" Elisa's green eyes blazed at me in the dim room. "I'm not going crazy. She was there. In the car."

I sat back. "You saw her down there? In the car?" Hard to sound believing, but I was trying.

"Of course I didn't *see* her. Have you ever been down that far underwater, where it's so dark, darker than night, darker than anything, and there's this whistling in your ears, and you claw in front of you, afraid you'll touch something? I touched the car. I felt the door handle and I was so terrified, because I knew they were still in there, the two of them, and I pushed off, on the roof, with my feet and a hand came out of where the window used to be . . . You've never . . ."

"You couldn't see but you know it was a hand that came out. You don't think you could have just caught your foot on the window glass or something?"

Elisa slumped back and closed her eyes. "It was a hand. Her hand."

I wondered what I should do. Call her mother? Or dial 911 and get an ambulance? Maybe even Dr. Manriquez, except he probably wouldn't talk to me because of patient privacy. I glanced cautiously at Elisa. She was looking at me.

"She said she wanted me to stay," Elisa whispered.

The hairs on my arms began to rise. Elisa had really flipped out.

"She said, 'Stay with us.' And she was holding my ankle. And then she said, 'Please.' "

I coughed to give myself time. "You could hear the words? Underwater?"

"Yes, I could hear the words. Didn't I just tell you? I kicked at her. But it's hard to kick underwater, Dru. It's like slow motion. And then I shook my foot and I felt it come free and I thought I was going to die because I'd been down there so long, and it was so dark, and I had no breath and it hurt so bad . . . it hurt so bad . . ."

I stroked her hair. "What hurt, Elisa?"

"Here." She touched her chest. "But then, somehow I was up, and you were all there, and Scooter. The boot came off, you see. She was left with it, and then she let it go." Tears had pooled in the corners of her eyes, and I pulled a tissue from the box on the table and dabbed them away.

"Did you tell Scooter?"

"Yes."

"What did he say?"

"What do you think? He said I should have brought her up with me. He said that would have been something to see." She hiccuped. "He thought it was pretty funny. But it's not, Dru. It's not."

"I know it's not."

I stood up, so mad at Scooter that if he'd been there I would have strangled him. Not because he didn't believe her. Because he'd left her like this.

Elisa clutched my hand. "Where are you going? If you call my mom I swear I'll never speak to you again as long as I live, Dru. Never." Her voice rose.

"I . . . I . . ." That was exactly what I'd planned on doing.

"And Scooter would be so mad at me. He wants me to be brave, like he is. To be perfect."

"Like he is," I said sarcastically. Elisa only nodded. Man! I stood looking down at her pale face. Maybe Mike and I could talk her into going to the emergency room at the hospital. But what would we say was wrong with her? This wasn't like a broken leg or a gash on her head. If I could only get her to relax and sleep.

"Where's Mike?" Elisa asked suddenly.

"He's waiting in the car," I said.

"Oh no. You mustn't make him wait. Never make him wait. Guys won't. I told Scooter, maybe sometime I'll jump with you, but it had to be now. It always has to be now." Her words ran together and she was getting hysterical again.

"I tell you what," I said. "I'll just run down and tell Mike you're okay, because we were both worried about you. All right?"

"Promise you won't call my mother."

"I promise."

"You don't think she'll come when you're gone, do you?"

"Your mother?"

"No. No. The girl in the car. The drowned girl."

"No chance," I said briskly. "The car's wedged. Remember, even the divers couldn't get her out."

Elisa closed her eyes. "That's right. That's why she wanted me to stay. They can't get out. They want company." She sighed. "And you'll come right back? When you've told Mike?"

"Definitely." I ran down the stairs.

The sun was almost gone and the sky was a deep crimson, but the air was warm still and it felt good. Mike looked good, too, coming out of the car, big, strong-shouldered, running his hand over his hair, speaking, saying ordinary things.

"Is she all right?' "

He held me while I told him how freaked out Elisa was. "And Scooter left her," I added. "He was in such a rush to get back to the glory . . ."

"Sh, sh!" Mike stroked my hair the way I'd stroked Elisa's. "No use us getting mad at him. He's the way he is. And Elisa knows it."

I pulled away a little. "What does that mean?"

He shrugged. "Just that opposites are supposed to attract, aren't they?"

"It's a mystery to me how Scooter attracts anyone," I said. "Whatever. I'm going to stay with Elisa until her mom gets back."

"I'll stay too," Mike said.

"No. She'd be afraid Scooter would find out."

"But—"

I put my fingers against his lips. "I've stayed in this house a bunch of times. She'll sleep, I think. And if she starts weirding out on me I'll call nine-one-one. I'll call her mom. I'll call *you*." It took some more talking before I got him persuaded.

I waited till he started up the car and turned the corner before I went back upstairs to Elisa.

She was almost asleep. I sat cross-legged on the floor beside her and held her hand until it dropped away from mine and I heard her breathing deeply.

The boot was all the way under the bed. I reached in, grabbed it, and carried it at arm's length straight out to the garbage can. Of course Elisa had been talking nonsense about the drowned girl asking her to stay. But even so, it was better to get rid of the thing. I put the lid tightly on the can. And then, I'm not sure why, I found a good-sized rock and put that on top, too.

SEVEN

ELISA WHIMPERED in her sleep and I waited till she settled. Then, as quietly as I could, I went back downstairs and called home.

"Hi, Dad. It's Dru. I'm going to be late. Elisa's not feeling well and her mom's at work. So I'm staying with her for a while."

"When do you think her mom will get back?"

"I don't know. Before midnight for sure. Mike said to call and he'll bring me home whenever." I kept my voice ordinary and cheerful and my mind away from Elisa's words: "She said she wanted me to stay. The drowned girl." My fingers clutched the receiver.

"Tell Elisa I hope she feels better," Dad said.

"I will."

I heard him yawn and knew I didn't want him to go. Dad, so real and safe and ordinary.

"Wait," I said. "Where's Mom?"

"She's showing that condominium on First Street again."

"Oh. And how was your day, Dad? Did you sell any pianos?"

"No. But I sold a penny whistle. Does that count?"

"It does with me." I stared at the faded hall wallpaper, with its fluffy clouds and faint outline of gulls. There'd been gulls today, screeching over the water, flapping in anger as Elisa and Scooter dropped past them.

"Anything exciting happen?" I asked Dad. "Any word from my big sister? She doesn't have a recital in Carnegie Hall or an offer from the Philharmonic?"

Dad laughed. " 'Fraid not."

I couldn't think of another reason to keep him talking. "Okay then. Bye, Dad."

"Goodnight, sweetie. Try not to be too late."

I hung up the phone and stood, listening again to the quiet, telling myself it was a good quiet. The longer Elisa slept the better. I fixed the phone to ring at its lowest volume and put it under one of the couch pillows.

The doorbell, loud and demanding, made me jump. Whoever was ringing it had a finger on the button and wasn't letting up.

I ran across the hallway and jerked open the door, ready to spit fire. Scooter stood there, smiling at me. He had changed into clean jeans and a dark blue knit shirt with white stripes on the collar. His face shone and his hair had dried into cute little curls loose and soft as a baby's around his head.

His smile faded when he saw me. "How come you're here? I told you Elisa was taking a nap and you didn't need to come over."

"She is taking a nap . . . was. I doubt if she is anymore."

Scooter gave me a blank look. "You mean she's still sleeping?"

"She *was*." I glanced back toward the stairs as Scooter stepped inside bellowing, "Elisa! Come on, baby. Rise and shine!"

"Are you *nuts?*" I asked him fiercely. "Don't you know the kind of state she's in?"

"Why don't you chill out," he said. His fists were clenched.

I took a step back, and then he looked past me and his voice changed. "Hi, babe!"

I glanced over my shoulder and there was Elisa, in the oversized sweatshirt, at the top of the stairs. I hadn't even noticed the shirt had a rainbow across the front. She held tightly on to the banister.

"Hey! Cute outfit!" Scooter made a kissing sound. "Come on down, doll, and give me a squeeze." He opened his arms wide. "And did you know that our names, yours and mine, are up on that board now for the whole world to see? Our little hearts, too. And I put two *x*'s. Kisses from me to you."

Elisa pushed back her tangle of hair. There were blue bruises big as thumbprints under her eyes.

I ran up the stairs. "How are you doing, Elisa?"

"I'm fine."

"Absolutely she's fine," Scooter said cheerfully. "All revived and ready to go again. Put some clothes on, though, will you, babe? We're partying."

I glared down at him. "Elisa's not up to partying tonight, Scooter. She's—"

Scooter leaned across the banister. "Who says she's not? What do you say, doll-face?"

Elisa shivered and hugged her arms around herself.

"I'm up to it," she said.

Scooter grinned. "Atta girl."

She stumbled toward her room, calling down, "Wait for me, okay? Wait, Scooter. I'll be quick."

I scowled at Scooter. "Are you sure you *can* wait? I hear you don't like to. Take off, why don't you?"

Elisa had changed course and veered toward the bathroom.

"You know what? I don't like bossy smart girls," Scooter said softly. He was still leaning across the banister in the hall, his chin resting on his folded arms. "And you know something else? What Elisa and I do is none of your business."

"We'll see."

I went over to the bathroom door and knocked on it. "It's Dru." Elisa let me in.

"Dru! Look at my hair. Do you think I have time to wash it? It's dried all weird. It's gone so curly and—"

"Oh, for Pete's sake, Elisa." I sat on the edge of the tub. "Quit worrying about your hair. You know, an hour ago you were so sick I was thinking seriously about taking you to the hospital."

Her laugh was high and fake. "The hospital? Just because I had a bad dream?" She leaned over, brushing her hair forward in a heavy curtain across her face. "Look okay?" she asked, shaking it back.

I sighed. "It looks fine."

She rushed to the bedroom and I followed her. "Be down in a minute, hon," she called loudly, then to me, "Find my red skirt, will you? It's in the closet. Maybe under something."

I found it and watched as she wriggled into it. I'd seen it before, short and tight as a second skin.

"Do you see my Cleopatra sandals?"

There were on the closet floor at the back.

"What's taking forever?" Scooter shouted up. "Need help?"

"He's getting mad, I can tell," Elisa said. "Maybe you should go down and tell him I need a few more minutes. I don't want him to see me up close looking like this." She smoothed blusher on her cheeks, leaning closer to the mirror. "I swear! Dracula's daughter!"

"You don't really want to go partying tonight, do you?" I asked. "If you stay, I'll stay with you till your mom comes. We can watch TV or play Scrabble. I bet I can still beat you at Scrabble."

"Are you serious? Do you think I'm going to let Scooter go without me? Especially tonight. All the girls will be grabbing for him, like Betsy. She's always analyzing him, playing doctor."

"You have till I count to ten," Scooter called. "Then you're history, Elisa. One, two . . ."

"How can you let him talk to you like that?" I said, my own face hot and burning. "He's a creep. You let him walk all over you."

Tom had said, "Elisa would do anything for Scooter."

Elisa reached for an eyebrow pencil. "You don't know him, Dru. He can be really sweet. Listen,

Dru. Thanks for being with me. I mean it. But forget all that stuff I said. Okay? I was just . . . upset."

"Eight . . . nine," Scooter called.

"Coming." Elisa grabbed her purse and hung it over her shoulder. She glanced at me and away. "Where's the boot? You know, the one that . . . that came off when we jumped." Oh so casual, so cool.

"I put it in the garbage can," I said. "I put a rock on top of the lid."

She didn't look at me. "Thanks, Dru."

I ran down the stairs behind her, almost bumping into her as she stopped, two steps from the bottom.

"Hey, Beautiful," Scooter said. He bent forward and kissed one of her bare, brown knees. I saw her shiver.

"At least take a jacket," I told Elisa, hating the way I sounded like somebody's mother. Mother hen, maybe.

"Aw, it's warm out." Scooter patted Elisa on the rear of the tight red skirt but it was me he smiled at—a smug smile. "Elisa's a strong, healthy girl."

"I guess she proved that today, all right," I said. Why was Elisa so gone on this loser, anyway? No use even asking myself. I knew part of it. Scooter was an in guy in school and even though school was over he'd be an in guy wherever he went. He was going to work in his dad's hardware shop—Navarro's: You Need It—We Have It—and he'd still be big stuff around La Paloma. Scooter was sure of himself, and exciting, and dangerous, all the things Elisa was not. Being with him meant never having time to be depressed. And probably when she looked at him she felt the way I feel when I look at Mike.

They were at the door now, ready to leave.

"You know, that jump was the biggest rush I ever got in my life," Scooter said. He had his hand on the back of Elisa's neck, and her hair tumbled over the sleeve of his shirt. "It's when you're free-falling, before you hit the water. Right, Elisa?"

"Right," she whispered.

"In fact,"—Scooter leaned forward to look into her face—"it's so incredible I want to do it again. You and me, babe. The first pair ever to challenge the Nail twice."

He couldn't be going to put Elisa through that again. She wouldn't do it, not after the ghost-girl thing. She wouldn't!

Elisa's eyes were closed. She looked like some- one who had been sick for a long, long time.

I took a deep breath, knowing that Scooter would love it if I started crabbing about another jump.

"Well," I said lightly, "maybe you could jump with Hopi and make it a threesome."

Scooter's lips tightened. "We're out of here. Time's a-wasting."

Elisa opened her eyes and looked at me. "Dru, how will you get home?"

"Mike said he'd come for me."

Elisa smiled shakily. "It's so neat, Dru. You and Mike."

I nodded.

"Sorry we can't offer you a ride." Scooter waved a hand. "My bike's just made for two. Oh, and if you guys want to come, we'll be at Spindrift." His eyes were big and innocent. "Diane already offered to call Mike to tell him where we'd be."

"Really?" I said. "She could have called me."

Scooter's hand was still on Elisa's neck under the tumble of her hair.

"I think she knows Mike's number," he said, and I knew from his sly smile that he was happy to hurt me.

"Bye, Dru," Elisa said. "I'm glad . . . thanks."

"Bye," I whispered. "Take care, Elisa."

I didn't go outside with them. Leaning against the inside of the front door I heard the scooter start up and roar away.

EIGHT

AFTER I CALLED MIKE I sat on the curb to wait for him. A huge potato bug was trying to make it up from the street to the sidewalk, probing with its antennae. I gave it a boost. Ten past eight now and the last light was going. I kept checking my watch, knowing Mike couldn't get here in less than twenty minutes, wishing he would. If I turned my head I could see the dented garbage can where I'd dumped the boot. I promised myself that I wouldn't look again. But I did.

When Mike drove up I yanked open the passenger door before he even stopped.

"Missed me *that* much?" he said grinning. "It's great it's so early. I thought you might have to stay for hours. Did Elisa's mom come home?"

"No." On the phone I'd just told him I was ready to leave. Now I explained.

"You don't mean Elisa and Scooter have gone to Spindrift?" he asked when I was through.

He knew about Spindrift, then. Diane *had* called

him. And I realized that he had changed clothes, too, that he was all shiny and scrubbed and showered just the way Scooter had been. His shorts were cream colored with a pale green stripe. His pale shirt had ironed creases, straight and crisp down the sleeves. Had he planned on going without me? What had he said to Diane? "Dru won't be able to make it. I'll leave a message where I'll be if she calls and I'll cruise by for a while." I bit my lip. What made me think he'd mentioned me at all?

"Do you want to drive over to Spindrift and check it out?" he asked, as he started up.

I looked down at my shorts and crumpled pink T-shirt. "In these?"

"Oh, you know that place. Nobody cares. Remember the night we were there and there was the guy in his baseball uniform?"

I smiled. "Remember the girl on roller skates? But still," I added.

"You look fine," Mike told me.

"Sure. How about changing shirts with me, then?"

Mike mock slowed the car. "I'm for that. Haul yours off."

"That's okay. If you take me home first I can change in two minutes."

"No problem."

I looked at him, at his brown arms with the little golden hairs, smooth as a baby lion's fur, at his hands, blunt fingered, the nails bitten like a little kid's. His nails always make me smile. The rest of him is so perfect. I probably like his nails best of anything about him.

We turned onto my street and stopped in front of our house, which looks as if it had been cloned from Elisa's, except that ours is a little better.

"You can always tell a house that's rented instead of owner occupied," Mom says with a sniff. "The property's just not kept up."

Dad gets defensive when Mom starts that stuff.

"It's the landlord who's supposed to keep it up," he says. "I don't see Bartholomew rushing over when we tell him the porch supports are eaten away by termites." Bartholomew's our twenty-three-year-old landlord. Our house is not owner occupied. But I don't think Mike cares.

"Do you know Scooter wants Elisa to jump with him again?" I asked. "Once is not enough."

"I heard that. But she won't, will she?"

He'd heard from Diane, of course.

"I don't know. The twins are probably taking bets on it. Do you want to come in?"

"No. I've got my book. I'm fine." And you won't even look at your watch, I thought. Nice Mike.

I ran inside and up the stairs. A Dodgers game was on the living room TV and I raised my voice over the announcer's.

"Dad? Elisa's okay and I'm going to Spindrift with Mike."

"All right. Don't be too late."

Already I was wondering what I'd wear. Normally that's not something I worry about too much. But things have changed since Mike. S.M., I call it. Since Mike and after Diane. She'd be dressed in some epic outfit. I pulled my T-shirt over my head as I rushed to the bathroom for a quick wash.

I found my peach-colored cotton shirt and my matching skirt that's not as tight or short as Elisa's and my white sandals with the cutouts in front.

"Kid shoes," Mike had teased the first time he saw them. "My little sister has a pair just like them." He'd hugged me and smiled. "Your legs are better, though. Hers are kind of spindly."

When he teased like that I trembled. Teasing was like touching, like a feather tickling your spine.

I pulled my hair back and up with a peach-colored ribbon. I'd worn it like this that wonderful night, the night Mike had first noticed me in the restaurant, standing there in the lobby with Dad on one side of me and Mom on the other, Mike across from us with his parents and his little sister, Janie.

"My birthday celebration," Mom had explained, flustered, her cheeks pink. "How nice to see you again after all these years, Sam. This is my husband, Andy, and our younger daughter, Dru. Our older daughter, Claire, is away at school." And then there had been introductions all around and Mike's dad saying, "I expect you two kids know each other already," and Mike looking at me, smiling, not the way he smiled, politely, when he met a bunch of us in the halls. Seriously looking at me now, seriously smiling, raising that one quizzical eyebrow. He'd moved to stand next to me. "Are you a ballet dancer?" he'd asked, and I'd laughed nervously before I realized he was serious. "Because of your hair," he'd said. "And the way you move." I'd put a hand up and touched my hair, and I'd shivered.

Our families hadn't been able to sit together. With every table filled it wasn't possible. But Mom had this gleam about her as if she'd been polished. "You're as beautiful as ever, Connie," Mr. Moriarty had told her. I guess that would shine a person up, all right. "Are you a ballet dancer . . . the way you move." That could shine a person up, too.

"What do you think, Dru?" Mom had asked. "Is Sam's wife older than he is?"

I'd pushed a cherry tomato around my salad plate. "I don't know. I think she looks nice."

"Yes." Mom had jabbed a circle of cucumber with her fork and held it up, staring at it as if she'd never seen cucumber before, and I'd glanced at her quickly.

Oh, Mom! Don't do this to Dad!

She had sighed. "Sam looks well. I heard he had heart surgery a while back but he looks well. Don't you think so?"

"He looks well," Dad had agreed.

The waiters and busboys all know us since Dad plays this room Saturday and Sunday nights. That's the reason we come. Fifteen percent off.

They would stop at our table. "Hi, Andy. How are you this evening? Nice to see you, Mrs. Driscoll. *Bonsoir*, Dru. *Guten Abend*." They liked to tease me with foreign language phrases since I was supposed to be such a whiz. A lot of the time they got it wrong. The hostess had stood talking to us for ages. Mom frowned, and I knew she didn't like it.

"It's okay, Connie," Dad had said, with mild sarcasm. "Your friends the Moriartys will just think we rate special attention."

"We do," I'd said, and Dad had smiled. "I like your hair that way, sweetie. You look like a flower."

"A flower with a pretty long stem," I'd said.

And now, with Mike waiting for me, I looked in the bathroom mirror and said, "Flower, huh?" But I felt good. How could I not with Mike waiting? And I told myself maybe I was worrying too much about Elisa. I'd keep an eye on her, the way I always did. I hummed a little tune under my breath and ran out, past the open door of my sister's room across the hall. On the bed lay the new clothes I'd take with me to Northwestern in the fall. The blue car coat, the fake Irish sweater my mom had bought at Buffums' sale. The short rain boots. I'd need them in Chicago. But no need to think about Northwestern or Chicago or fall now. It was summer and I was on my way to Spindrift, with Mike!

Mike leaned across to open the car door for me and smiled. "What color is that you're wearing? It's pretty."

"Peach."

"Oh. I thought it might be orange, but what do I know?" And then he added, "You fixed your hair the way I like it." I slid down in the seat, happy and filled with a soft warmth. Maybe I'd never wear my hair any other way again.

Spindrift is really just a wooden deck on short pilings on the beach. It has a wide sand-scuffed space for dancing, a jukebox that plays old tunes, romantic and sweet, and a long rough counter for serving hot dogs and hamburgers and soft drinks. Heaters on tall metal poles take the chill off the air, and one corner is glassed in as a protection from the ocean breezes. That's where the two warmest tables are, so that corner's always in demand. It looked as if it was ours for the evening. I saw Scooter and Elisa and Tweeny there and a lot of the kids who'd been at the jump today. Some of them I knew, some I didn't. I looked around for Lizzie, but she hadn't come.

Scooter had his arm around Elisa's shoulders, but he was talking to a girl in a white halter top who was perched on the edge of the table. She had long, sparkling earrings, and her eyes were wide with admiration as she hung on Scooter's words. Big man on campus, I thought. The girl and everybody here knew about the jump and figured him for a hero. And he was lapping it up.

"Good thing there's nobody over thirty," I said, and Mike asked, "What, Dru?"

"Nothing," I said.

Even from this far away I could see how pale Elisa was. I could see the two red blotches on her cheekbones where she'd stroked on the blusher.

Betsy was dancing with one of the McInerney twins and Diane with the other, the four of them close together on the crowded wooden floor.

It was Diane who spotted us first and started pushing toward us. "Hey, Mike! You got here," she called.

I got here, too, I thought. Thanks for noticing. But she was noticing all right, checking me out with cool eyes. Okay, I was checking her out, too. She was wearing stone-washed jean shorts, so faded they were almost white, with red suspenders and a red-and-white-checked shirt. The simple country look, but not really. Behind her I saw Tom McInerney, still standing on the dance floor, his hands spread out in a what-happened-she-was-here-a-minute-ago gesture. There was a look on his face I'd never seen before. Hurt? Teed off? I couldn't decide, but I knew I felt sorry for him. It wasn't hard to see Diane would dump him in a minute if she thought she could get Mike back.

"We weren't sure you would make it." She gave us a dazzling smile, first Mike, then me.

You mean, you hoped I wouldn't, I thought. "We made it," I said.

Mike glanced down at me. "You know what, Dru, you must be starved. You didn't have any dinner, did you?"

"Huh-uh." I shook my head.

"Like a hamburger?" he asked, and Diane said, "We saved you two seats at the table, just in case. Go on over when you get your food." She lowered her voice. "Wait till you see what we've planned for Scooter later." She looked quickly at me and added, "For Elisa, too, of course."

"Is she okay?" I asked.

Diane sounded impatient. "She's great. In fact, she and the Scoot are going to jump again."

I felt as if I were smothering. "Is it for sure? When?"

Diane shrugged. "*I* don't know."

Mike touched my hand. "I'll get your hamburger and drink. You go on over to the table, Dru."

"Thanks." I edged diagonally across the sanded floor to the corner. Outside, the spotlights mounted on the sides of Spindrift turned the waves to black gold and the beach at the water's edge to silver. Beyond was the deep ocean darkness, blacker than night and filled with secrets.

"Hi, Dru." The group around the table parted to let me through . . . one of the in crowd—a friend of the heroes. Tweeny squeezed over to make room for me between her and Scooter. Elisa was on the end, beside him and next to the glassed-in V of the corner. I could see her reflection, two Elisas, both sitting stiff and rigid. I didn't even look at Scooter as I sat down and leaned forward.

"How are you doing, Elisa?"

Scooter answered for her. "She's terrific." He put his hand on the back of her neck again, under her hair. That seemed to be his favorite caress, if it was a caress. Maybe it made him feel in control, like a puppet master. He kissed her cheek and smiled around at his admirers. "You should have seen this lady today. Just took my hand and leaped with me into the great unknown."

The girl in the white jersey halter top put her elbows on the table and leaned across it. Her ear-rings dangled to her shoulders and shot off pin-points of light.

"Just ask any girl here. Any one of us would jump with you, Scooter."

Scooter grinned. "No offense, Maria. You know the old saying 'Look before you leap'? Nine-tenths of the lookers are never going to leap, I guarantee you that."

Maria nodded. "I guess."

"Yep. Many are called but few are chosen," Scooter said. Oh, was he enjoying himself! Was I the only one who thought he was sickening, mouthing off like this?

"*Elisa* was chosen," I said, wishing I could sit next to her, wishing I could even see her, which I couldn't with Scooter between us. All I could see were her hands, gripping the edge of the table.

Scooter turned and his lips brushed her hair. "Chosen by me, right, baby?"

"Right," Elisa whispered.

Scooter peered around restlessly. "Hey!" He grinned. "Look at Hopi and Diane, would you? Is this a new thing or what?"

The crowd around him turned to look.

I looked too. There was Diane dancing now with Hopi, her hair spilling silver across his black-shirted chest as she leaned against him, the two of them almost motionless as they swayed to the music. Diane lifted her face and Hopi leaned forward so their lips touched.

"I *tell* you," Scooter shouted, smacking his hand on the table, "the whole world loves a jumper."

"What do you mean?" That was Maria of the dangling earrings asking.

"Hopi's the next one who's going to jump the Nail," Tweeny offered, and I heard the awe in her voice.

"No kidding?" Maria asked. "I sure love his fringed boots!"

Scooter scowled. "He hasn't jumped yet. Talk comes easy. He *says* he's going to jump. He hasn't looked over the edge yet himself."

"I think he did look today," Tweeny said, "when he was putting your names up on the board."

Maria straightened the top of her halter. "He's pretty cute. Maybe I'll just cut in."

"On Diane Skoal?" Tweeny sounded shocked. "Nobody cuts in on her."

I did, I thought. And where was Tom McInerney, now that Diane was with Hopi? He was standing by the jukebox, his twin beside him. They were talking, looking not at each other but at Hopi and Diane on the dance floor. Betsy stood with them looking bored. I thought the McInerneys were probably talking "twin talk," the speech that only they understood. Tom still had a hurt look on his face. Behind them I saw Mike at the counter putting the hamburgers and drinks into a cardboard carrying box. He wouldn't care that Diane was with Hopi, or Tom, or anyone, would he?

Now Tweeny was defending herself to Scooter. "Hopi said it was all right to tell about his jump."

"You yak too much," Scooter said. "Yak, yak, yak."

Tweeny's face got pink. "You started it, Scooter. You said the whole world loves a jumper. And then I said—"

Scooter scowled. "I know what you said." It almost made me laugh. Scooter was not into sharing any of the glory.

Elisa put her hand on his arm. "Could you get me another lemonade, Scooter? I have this terrible thirst."

And I realized those were just about the first words she'd spoken since I'd come to the table. She wasn't all right, whatever she said, whatever anyone said.

"Sure. Coming right up, babe." Tweeny got a last, hard look as Scooter left. She got up, too. "I'm going over to talk to Betsy," she said. "That guy has a super-bad temper, Elisa. He's scary."

Elisa shrugged. "Not to me." Her gaze followed Scooter as he pushed to the counter. "Look at all those girls crowding him," she whispered. "They're like a swarm of mosquitoes. I told you they would be, Dru. Any one of them would jump with him if I didn't. You heard them, Dru."

"Oh Elisa! For Pete's sake . . ."

Elisa bit her lip. "I know you don't like him, either, Dru, but—"

I interrupted. "I don't like what he's doing to you. You're not going to jump again? Tell me you're not."

On the dance floor kids were weaving together, dreamy and romantic. Diane had both arms around Hopi's neck, her hands clasped behind his head. His thumbs were hooked in her red suspenders. Some guy with a raspy voice was singing "Stardust," and the old record jumped every time the needle came around to the scratch.

Elisa clutched my hand. "Dru? Don't tell anybody else! Promise you won't. I know you keep your promises and I have to tell you." Her voice lowered. "She's out there. Now."

My heart started a slow, heavy beat. "Who? Out where?" As if I didn't know.

"The drowned girl. There she is. Look! Look!" Elisa was staring through the glass that was blurred by spray and sea fog, and I stared, too. There was nothing out there except the waves leaving their creamy trail on the sand and the wind blowing through the ice plant by Spindrift. And us. Our cloudy reflections.

I turned toward Elisa and saw that that's what she was looking at. Us.

"That's *you*, goony," I said. "And that's me behind you. Hi, hi!" I waved. In the glass I waved back at myself, grinning an oily grin. "See?"

"I see," Elisa said. "I see the drowned girl."

NINE

By THE TIME MIKE brought our food Scooter was back.

"Let's move to another table where there's more room," I told Mike, and I tried to pretend that I was enjoying the hamburger. But I didn't feel like eating. I could still hear Elisa's trembling voice saying, "She's out there," and though my back was toward her now, I felt the chill of her frightened eyes. We were facing the floor space where Diane and Hopi danced. If danced was the word. I thought Spindrift was like a stage with one spotlight on the two of them and another on the McInerney twins, still standing by the jukebox, both of them grim. It was always that way with the twins. When one hurt, the other did, too. Behind us were Elisa and Scooter with his admirers, and beyond them the glass and . . . and what? Nothing. No one.

I forced myself to take another bite of the burger. "This is good," I told Mike. "Thanks."

When he didn't answer I glanced up at him. He

was watching two guys building a tower of playing cards, but he must have been looking at Diane, too, because he said, "Seems like Diane has a new interest."

I nodded.

"I'm not all that surprised," Mike said. "Tom always acted hotter for her than she was for him. And besides, he'll be heading off for Penn State in September and then it'll be all over, anyway."

I pushed aside the rest of my food. "Diane's heading off too, for San Diego, and Hopi will be staying here. So if anything starts with them it'll be over fast, too."

"Naw. San Diego's close. She'll see Hopi all the time. But old Tom will be long gone."

So will I, I thought. And you and Diane will see each other all the time. I turned my head away.

"Do you want to walk on the beach?" Mike asked.

I nodded. "Yes, please," I said. "I'd like to walk."

We passed the other table.

"Wait, Dru, where are you going?" Elisa half rose from her seat and her voice got louder. "Don't go out there, Dru."

"It's okay," I told her. "It's okay, Elisa. Mike's with me."

She put her hand over her mouth and began shaking her head.

"I won't be cold," I added, so the others would think that's what she'd meant.

"Come to think of it, you might be cold," Mike said. "I'll get you my jacket from the car."

I stood on the steps outside Spindrift waiting as he ran across to the parking lot, and I didn't let myself look back inside at Elisa or into the darkness beyond the lights. Even though I knew there was no drowned girl there, I watched only Mike, his shadow running beside him toward his car. Then he was back, his leather bomber jacket over his arm.

He helped me put it on and pulled the fur collar up around my throat.

"Good fit," he said and smiled that smile that somersaults my heart.

We stopped beyond Spindrift's brightness. Mike turned me to face him, his hands warm on my back under the jacket, his lips warm on mine. He kissed my closed eyes, held me so tight against him that it hurt. When I'd fantasized about a boy like Mike, I'd believed kisses would be enough. I'd never thought my way through to the other side, not until graduation night. Not until Murchisons. That was the first time I'd known this terrible urgency.

There'd been a big, all-night graduation blast for seniors up at the country club. Mike and I'd snuck away. There's a cliff walk called Murchisons . . . such an ordinary name for such a magical place. Once, before it became a state park, the Murchison family had a house on the point. They'd planted bougainvillea and dark red fuchsia and small, squat palm trees. When the state took it over the Murchisons had to move out and the house lay empty. Vandals started a fire one night and now there were just tumbled walls covered with the flowering vines. The palm trees had grown tall, bent over now with the winds. Mike had driven us there and I'd hiked up my dress and we'd climbed the wire fence into park property. He spread the blanket he keeps in the car and we sat in what had once been the Murchisons' front yard, the smells of wild honeysuckle and jasmine lifting around us, the moon making a shivering path across the sea, and we'd kissed and touched each other, and my heart had been beating so fast and so hard that it scared me. Was this what love was, this fluttering frightened wanting? We'd lain down on the blanket and sometime, then or later, I'd held Mike away and said, "I don't want to do this, Mike. I don't."

And he'd leaned on his elbow, the sky and a million stars behind him, and he'd said softly, "You don't have to do anything you don't want to, sweetheart. Not with me. Not ever."

We'd sat up, our arms around each other, looking across the molten darkness of the sea and I'd been filled with so much wonder and happiness. Was this love, I'd wondered.

Standing now on the Spindrift beach with Mike I knew that urgency was a part of love. My heart pounded against him, against that pale shirt that smelled of Tide or Cheer or something just as clean and fresh. Against the pounding of him.

"Do you know how much time we have left?" he whispered, kissing me again. "Do you know?"

I tried to say that I didn't, not exactly, but there was no way to speak.

"Not even three months," he said. "Then you go in one direction and I go in the other. I told my parents today that I didn't want to go with them on vacation. If I went we'd lose two whole weeks together."

"Oh, Mike!"

"Do you know how far it is from Chicago to San Diego?"

"No." I breathed the word into the warm hollow

of his neck. Sad, lonely music drifted from Spin-drift.

"A long, long way," he said.

My voice shook. "I'll be home for vacations. You'll be home, too. We'll see each other."

"Don't go," he whispered.

"What?" I tried to pull away.

"Don't go to Chicago." The words came, each punctuated by a kiss. "Stay here. Stay with me. Come to San Diego State. It's a great school. Good foreign language department."

"I know that." I tried to laugh. "But you're not serious. Great schools cost. I've got a scholarship, Mike. That's how come I can go at all."

Strands of my hair drifted down and blew across my face. Mike tried to tuck them back.

"I know. I'm not serious. I just wish you didn't have to leave, that's all."

"I wish that, too, in a way. Which is weird, because I've always wanted to go away to college, to get an education. That's what Claire and I both wanted. That's what I still want, but . . ."

"You know what my dad said today?" Mike was rubbing his arms as if he were cold, and I opened the leather jacket and said, "Here! Come in here with me."

I held the warmth around both of us. "Your dad said . . . ?"

"He said, 'Don't let your Dru go. I made that mistake with her mother.' "

"What?" I couldn't believe it. "But his wife, I mean, your mother, she's so nice and . . ."

"He doesn't think about your mom now, I'm pretty sure of that," Mike said. "But seeing her that night in the restaurant brought it all back. He sounded sad, Dru. He said, 'I suppose everybody has a love that gets away.' "

It was so warm now inside the coat, so warm with our bodies close like this, our faces touching.

"I just don't want it to be that way for us, Dru. I don't want to be old and saying, Once I had a love and she got away."

A love and she got away. It was so sad.

"Oh, Mike." I traced a finger down the hard curve of his cheek, around his lips. Was he saying he loved me? Was that what he meant? I knew one thing, being close like this, the heat between us, the blood moving so quickly through every pulse, was scary—scary and exciting and dangerous. My legs were crumpling. In another second Mike and I would be folded together on the cold, feathery sand, the coat over us, and it would be the way it had been that night up at Murchisons except that it would be harder now for both of us to stop. We wouldn't be able to. We wouldn't want to.

Someone was calling us, a voice, two voices struggling to be heard over the crashing of the surf and the pull of the night wind.

"Mike! Dru!"

We moved apart. "Who is it?" Mike sounded so furious it made me smile. In the nick of time, I thought, whatever a nick of time was. We turned together, the coat still holding us, and I saw two girl shapes on the steps of Spindrift, Betsy and Tweeny, windmilling their arms to get our attention. "Come . . . missing . . . hurry." A word here and there reached us while the wind tossed the others away.

"We're being summoned," I said.

"I know. I can tell," he muttered, so grumpy it made me smile again. "They look like they're guiding an airplane in for landing. What do they want us for, anyway?"

"Probably for the celebration," I said. "You know, the one for Scooter. Scooter *and* Elisa. Diane told us. Remember?"

"I don't even *want* to go to a celebration," Mike said loudly, and I tugged gently at his jacket till I had it all to myself again, and said, "Oh yes, you do. It's cold out here. And besides. It's just in the nick of time."

Mike smiled. "You're not kidding!"

I smiled, too, and I felt smug and happy. Mike didn't want to go in to the celebration Diane had planned. He wanted to stay here with me. I ran my hand down his arm. "See? You're all goose bumps! Let's run."

He took my hand and we ran a few steps in the sand, but it was hard going and pretty soon we slowed. Betsy and Tweeny had disappeared inside. Earlier I'd thought the dance floor was like a lighted stage but now it seemed to me that the whole of Spindrift was a wonderful brightly lit ship, sailing across a dark sea, romantic and magical. I knew it was being with Mike that made it that way.

I put my head close to his. "We still have plenty of nights. Not many days, though. Remember, I start work next week. And you'll be going to the sites with your dad."

Something moved in the shadows by the wooden pilings. The muscles in my neck tightened. "What's that over there?"

We stared into darkness made blacker by the

lights around it. "It's a man," Mike said. "A person, anyway."

"Oh no," I whispered, thinking of the drowned girl. Drowned, dead, under the sea.

"It's all right," Mike whispered. "It's probably just someone who's come to sleep on the beach."

We were moving again, closer to Spindrift and the seated figure. Now I could see that it was a woman sitting on the sand, wrapped in a dark blanket that came right up over her head. She was eating a hot dog. Sand blew on the shallow Spindrift box beside her and across her blanketed legs. She took a sip from one of the Spindrift's paper cups. On her other side was a canvas bag, shapeless and big as a suitcase. Something small and red was propped on top of it, and as we got closer I saw that it was a little radio with a bent aerial.

"Homeless," Mike whispered. "The guys in Spindrift probably give her free food. Could be she hangs around here every night."

I shivered. "How awful. And it's so cold and damp and . . ."

"I know," Mike said. "I swear if I were a billionaire I'd build houses for everybody."

"Should we say anything to her?" I whispered.

"Like what?" But Mike spoke as soon as we were

level with her. "How are you doing? Getting enough to eat there?"

Now I could see her face plainly, old, or maybe not so old, just tired and lined.

"I could use another cup of coffee," she said, and Mike nodded. "I'll get you one."

"Could you stay with me for a while?" she asked.

"Maybe not right now. But I'll come back with your coffee." His hand on my arm urged me on.

"I drink it black," the voice called after us.

We stopped on the bottom step. "Oh, Mike, I wish . . . we could do something."

"I know," he said gently.

Tweeny and Betsy appeared from the shelter of Spindrift's glass.

"Get a move on, you two. Diane's just about ready to go."

"Go where?" Mike asked. "I'll get that coffee," he said to me.

"Come on!" Tweeny's voice was shrill. "Diane won't start till Mike's there."

"Why not?" I asked. "I thought this big event was for Elisa and Scooter." I sat on the step and unbuckled one of my sandals. The little openings had let in half the beach. I poured it out, took off the other sandal, and saw Mike coming from the counter with the coffee and two doughnuts in a paper napkin.

"Wait for me," he said, going carefully down the steps. Did he think I wouldn't?

I sat, hugging my knees, thinking that of course it had been the poor homeless person that Elisa had seen. The woman probably looked in and for a second Elisa had glimpsed the shape of her, not really seeing her face because of the misty glass and her own terror. It was a relief to know that Elisa had seen *someone,* not just a reflection, and that she hadn't totally flipped out.

"She just made a mistake," I said out loud to a snail who was making his slow way across the step to the shelter of the ice plant.

Mike seemed to have been gone for a long time, and then he was back, smiling down at me.

"That was nice of you," I said.

"I am nice. I keep telling you." He was teasing again and it was good and easy and normal, our pulses calmed.

"Her name's Virginia," he said. "She sleeps under Spindrift and she has a piece of plywood propped up in there for a windbreak. She says it's not bad. She likes the music, and when the jukebox stops at night she plays her radio."

"You did stay and talk to her," I said softly, and he shrugged. "Not for long."

Betsy poked her head around the glass and said, "People who keep other people waiting are basically insecure. It gives them a false feeling of importance."

"That's interesting, Betsy." Mike winked at me, and we went up the last of the steps.

Spindrift buzzed with talk and laughter. The dance floor was crowded, and on the jukebox a woman sang about cheating hearts. I wanted to get next to Elisa and reassure her that the only person on the beach was Virginia and that it was Virginia she'd seen. I looked across at the table. Elisa was still next to the glass with Scooter. On his other side was Maria, her earrings swinging in sparkling arcs as she leaned close to whisper something in his ear. Scooter laughed. I heard him say in a loud voice, "Diane's planning something extra special for our celebration. I can feel it in my bones."

It would be extra special. And Elisa and Scooter wouldn't be the stars, Diane would. I felt that in my bones.

TEN

SOMEONE PULLED THE PLUG on the jukebox and the dancers came to a bewildered stop. The servers and the short-order cook left what they were doing and leaned across the counter to find out what was going on. And then Betsy, over by Spindrift's entrance, sang out, "Everybody's here, Diane. We're ready."

Including Mike, I thought.

A door opened. I don't know where it led to— a storage room probably.

Diane Skoal stepped out.

I caught my breath.

Around me were murmurs of admiration and surprise. The dancers shuffled back to stand in a ring on the outside of the dance floor as if the whole scene had been set up by a movie director, and I was thinking again, It's a stage. And the spot light is on Diane now. Just the way she wants it to be.

She wore a long gleam of a dress covered with

green sequins. Her hair was garlanded with a shining green wreath, the gold and green ribbons attached to it cascading down her back.

She walked slowly onto the dance floor, the green sheath shimmering at every step. I thought she looked pretty ridiculous, but beautiful, too.

"Where did she find the mermaid getup?" Mike whispered. I shook my head.

Everything was quiet except for the sigh of the sea outside, the small rattle of the glass walls, and the smooth slide of Diane's slippers as she crossed the wooden floor. Her hands were behind her.

Tom McInerney, over by the counter, had taken a step toward her, but his twin grabbed his arm and held him back. Hopi stood with his friends close to the glass walls, and I could see how tense he was, his head pushed forward like the head of the snake tattooed on his arm.

Diane stopped in the center of the floor.

"I command the King and Queen of the Deep to step forward," she said.

There was some giggling and shoving. Beside me Mike muttered, "Spare us!" I gave him an amused glance and saw that he was biting his nails. I knew he did that, but I'd never seen him in action. Probably only in times of stress, I thought, and then I thought, How could anybody see Diane looking like this and not want her? How could he not be remembering?

"Scooter! Elisa! The mermaid's talking to you," Betsy said, and Mike murmured, "Don't keep her waiting. That's a sign of basic insecurity." It was nice that he could joke. But he was still nibbling at his thumbnail.

"You're the King and Queen of the Deep," Tweeny giggled. "Step forward, Your Majesties."

I turned and saw Scooter rising, pulling on Elisa's hand to bring her up with him. She was holding on to the table, shaking her head. Behind her, on the other side of the glass, was the pale outline of a face. Virginia! From here she could have been a blurred ghost picture, only her head visible above the dark swathe of blanket. If Elisa saw her she'd freak.

I moved quickly to the end of the table. "They want *you*, Elisa," I said, "but you don't want to go, do you? It's so dumb." My voice forced her to look in my direction. "You don't want to be Queen for a day . . . or a week, even. Not if it's a part of that stupid jump."

Elisa was stumbling toward me now, her blank stare fixed on me, not on the glitter of the green mermaid or the night outside. I held out my hand, ignoring Scooter's frown and his muttered, "Butt out, will you?"

"Scooter!" That was Maria. "If Elisa doesn't want to go with you, I'll stand in for her."

"Naw," Scooter said. "Elisa's all right."

Somebody in the crowd whispered loudly, "Is she *drunk?*"

Elisa had found my outstretched hand and clutched at it.

"Come on," I whispered. "Come for a drive with Mike and me. I know—*Guys and Dolls* is playing at the Rialto. Remember when we were both in *Guys and Dolls* at school?" I was holding her up, easing her out. Then Scooter was beside me, taking Elisa's arm.

"I think the mermaid wants the King and Queen to come up front, Dru. I don't think she wants any hangers-on."

"Oh, Scoot . . . Dru's my friend . . . how *can* you?" Elisa whispered.

That's not the question, I thought. It's how can you, Elisa? How can you stand this creep?

Scooter pried her fingers from mine and said, "Come on up with me and be a heroine, babe." He led her away. Her T-shirt had come out of the skirt band in back and I wished I could at least fix it for her, but I couldn't. She was beyond my reach now. A glance over my shoulder showed me that Virginia was still out there, still enjoying the show. I moved so I stood between her and Elisa but I knew Virginia would move, too, not allowing her view to be blocked off. For her this entertainment would help pass the night. It would be almost as good as someone staying to visit. She took a few steps to the side, pressing her face against the glass, and I took a few steps, too, both of us doing some strange dance, one on the inside, the other outside.

"You're not going to ask us to kneel, are you?" Scooter asked Diane, laughing but serious, too. I decided she better *not* ask him to kneel.

"That won't be necessary." Diane was standing there like Miss California, Miss America, Miss Everything. Her eyes flicked toward Mike and she smiled a mysterious smile. "Now," she said and brought from behind her back two wreaths made from dried, dark seaweed. I drew in a breath. The wreaths would have that salty medicinal smell you get on the beach after a storm or when you jog in the soft sand high above the tidemark.

Elisa gave a little moan as Diane put one of

the seaweed wreaths on her head, the other on Scooter's.

"I crown you King and Queen of the Deep," Diane said,

There was a moment's silence; then Scooter said, "My lady and I accept the honor."

Through the hooting and applause came Tweeny's high, reedy voice. "You can thank Betsy and me for your crowns. We gathered the stuff this morning, jumping the gun, so to speak."

"Jumping the jump," Scooter corrected, looking around for appreciation of his pun.

Tweeny shuddered. "Wow! You should have seen the flies in the seaweed! And all those little shell things, like worms. We had to pick them out."

"Oh, yuk!" someone said.

"They're fine now," Tweeny added quickly with a glance at Betsy's irritated face. "Betsy and I washed the stuff off."

Scooter and Elisa were trying to get back to the table, Elisa white and shaken, the wreath crooked on her red hair. Virginia was still by the glass. I moved again to block her dark shape.

"Just call us Your Majesties and bow as we pass," Scooter told the crowd, and he laughed and said, "Bless you, my child," as a girl in a flowered sundress held out her skirt and curtsied.

"Now he thinks he's the Pope," Mike muttered.

But something else was happening on the deck of Spindrift. Hopi had pushed through the circle to stand with Diane. They looked so odd together, so mismatched. And Tom McInerney was trying to get to her, too. His twin shouldered him back, like someone blocking a basketball shot. Hopi whispered to Diane and she smiled. Slowly she took the glittering garland from her head and put it on his. It should have looked stupid, perched there above the red headband that circled his forehead, the streamers dangling down the back of his black shirt, but somehow it didn't. Hopi has this sort of power. He has his own kind of dignity.

The jukebox had been plugged in again and the singer had taken up where she left off. "You'll cry and cry and try to sleep," she wailed. Hopi and Diane danced, moving together so intimately it was embarrassing to watch.

"Wow! Scorch!" one of Hopi's friends said, shaking his hand as if he'd been burned, and around us kids began jeering and whistling and stamping their feet. Spindrift trembled.

And then, as abruptly as it had started, the music stopped again. Beside the jukebox, holding the dangling wire and plug, was Grant McInerney. His twin stood next to him.

"My brother has an announcement," Grant said, and Tom held up both arms for silence.

"Grant and I will jump the Nail together—tonight!" he shouted.

Voices erupted into the silence.

"What?"

"At night? Are you crazy?"

"Fantastic! Nail it!"

"Don't be stupid, Tom." That was Mike, shouting above everyone. "You won't be able to see what you're doing. Do you want to get yourselves killed?"

"We're jumping tonight." Tom didn't even look at Diane, but I did. She was smiling in that faint, mysterious way again. I knew Tom was jumping because of her. And Elisa had jumped because of Scooter. There was something wrong here, something really, really wrong. No person should have that much control over another person's life.

"Here it comes," Scooter said in a bored voice. "The first of the copycats."

"The ritual is wrong," Hopi said. "It's too soon. You shouldn't buck the ritual."

"I don't give a jack bull diddley about the ritual," Tom said. "We're jumping now. And you're all invited to come watch."

ELEVEN

THE CARS WERE FULL for the single-file drive
along Coast Highway. "Like a wedding," I said to
Mike.

"Or a funeral. Except for the noise." He nodded
toward the front of the procession where Scooter
and Elisa led the way on the little red bike. Mike
and I were alone in his car. Till the last minute I'd
tried to get Elisa and Scooter to drive with us.

"She's tired," I'd told Scooter. "This way she
can sit in the back and close her eyes."

"She goes with me," Scooter said.

In the headlights of the other cars I saw that
he and Elisa both had on their helmets and that
the seaweed wreaths dangled, windblown, from
Scooter's wrist.

"I still wish we didn't have to go watch this," I
told Mike.

"It's not too late to turn around," he said. "Except . . . you did promise Elisa."

"I know."

I'd made the promise in the line in the women's rest room at Spindrift, Elisa's trembling lips close to my ear.

"I have to go, Dru. And I'm so scared. Please come too. Please . . . please." The pleases sounded as if they could go on forever.

"But *why* do you have to go?" I'd asked, and she'd shot a quick glance at Maria, who was at the mirror, adding another layer of scarlet lipstick to her scarlet lips, watching us in the mirror as we whispered together. Maria leaned closer to her reflection, checked her eye makeup, tested the flick of her sparkling earrings, hummed under her breath.

Elisa and I edged up as the line shortened. "With guys like Scooter—Mike too—there are always girls who want to push you aside and move in," Elisa had said.

"But . . . we can't be watchdogs all our lives. If a guy cares about you, you shouldn't have to keep proving stuff." Suddenly I was thinking about Diane Skoal and about how unsure I always was when she was around. What gave me the right to lecture Elisa?

"Sit close to me at the jump," Elisa had begged. "What if the drowned girl gets the twins? It'll be my fault . . . I should warn them."

"Sh!" Her voice was rising, and I'd nodded back toward Mariam who had joined the end of the line. "You don't want her to hear you. I'll talk to the twins."

"But don't tell them I said—"

"I won't." So senseless, everything senseless. One minute Elisa was going to warn them herself. The next she didn't want me to mention her name. And what was I to say anyhow? "There's a dead girl down there, and she's going to want you to stay?" Tom McInerney would think I'd lost it completely.

I'd cornered the twins at their car. Tom said they were waiting for Diane, who was changing out of her mermaid dress. He looked happy. Well, he had what he wanted. Diane's attention. But he still has to jump, I'd thought. Scooter was right about that. It's not enough just to say you're going to.

Grant was fidgeting, rubbing off a dried-up glob of bird dirt on the roof, pulling at an old decal on the windshield that was half gone. Poor Grant. He was probably scared out of his mind. But there was no way he'd let his twin jump alone.

"Look," I'd started. "Tom! I know you're set on this craziness. But just think—if you get hurt, it's the end of everything for you. Diane won't want you if you're paralyzed and lying out in Rancho

Los Amigos, or if you're *dead*. And now Grant's stuck with jumping, too."

"Grant doesn't have to," Tom had said. "I told him that already." He was looking past me, watching for Diane.

"Elisa described to me how . . . how terrible it is to jump." I wasn't sure how to put this. "You go so far underwater, and there are things down there that you can get snagged on. There's that old car. Elisa's foot got caught in it . . . on it." I swallowed, trying to find the right words.

But it hadn't mattered. Diane came out of Spindrift, the green mermaid dress tossed over her arm. On her hair was the glittering green wreath, the one she'd put on Hopi's head. She'd taken it back. Tom smiled, and I knew he'd noticed the wreath, too. I was struck again by the power of girls like Diane. And maybe the determination, too, if they didn't get what they wanted. I took a deep breath. Mike! Mike and Diane in San Diego. Me in Chicago. And I remembered my own words, "We can't be watchdogs all our lives."

"All set?" Tom opened the passenger door for Diane the way a footman would for a princess.

"Are *you* all set?" She'd tossed the dress in back, then stood on tiptoe to kiss Tom's nose.

He'd grinned. "I'm ready for anything."

Stopping him had been hopeless from the start, but I'd promised Elisa I'd try. I'd promised I'd go. And now Mike was slowing, turning onto the dirt road that led to the base of the Nail.

"Last chance," he said. "Once we get in here we're trapped."

"Keep going," I whispered.

We were the fourth car in. Ahead of us and behind us headlights shone across the black rocks. I saw Scooter and Elisa, the bike bumping all the way to the water's edge. The black surface of the Deep, even more terrifying at night than in the daytime, looked like oil. You could imagine all kinds of things down there, sliding up from another world.

Elisa stood gazing down into it as if she saw and heard those things that the rest of us could only imagine. Everyone kept their headlights on, even with the cars stopped. I couldn't decide if the beams of light made it better or worse. They might help the twins see the water. Or they might blind them as they dropped. From here, the lights stopping abruptly at the bottom, the cliffs dark above them, they added to the horror. I thought of the lone car of the McInerney twins up there on top buffeted by the wind. Above the Nail there was a faint shining, maybe the headlights of their Honda directed toward the cliff's edge at the place where the leap would begin, reflecting upward into the sky. There'd be no light, though, in the gaping blackness of space below. I held on to the car seat on either side of me, as dizzy as if I were the one about to fall.

Behind us Diane got out of Betsy's car and Tweeny followed her. Diane had changed transportation at the entrance. I'd watched in the rearview mirror as she gave Tom a kiss and a cheery wave. He might have been going off to play football.

Tweeny knocked on Mike's window. "Come on, you two. Don't be late for the performance."

"That girl is a total idiot," Mike said.

"I have to go over and hold on to Elisa, anyway," I said. "Look at her. Why isn't Scooter watching out for her? She's so close to the edge, if she slips she'll be in the Deep herself."

I opened the car door. It was cold outside, cold, and a wind blew through the little weeds that grew in the crevices of the cliffs. It rattled an empty soda can across the rocks and into a tide pool. I'd taken off Mike's jacket and he leaned in back to get it.

"Here, Dru."

"But what about you?"

"I'll be fine."

How odd that the wind blew like this and yet the surface of the Deep was unruffled, moving only in that hypnotic in-and-out slide. How odd, too, that though Diane stood on the path with Betsy and Tweeny, Hopi didn't go near them. Hopi was strange. Maybe he stayed away from her out of a sense of fairness. This was Tom's night to do the proving. Hopi would stay out of it. Or maybe he and Diane had quarreled about who she drove with tonight, whose girl she was, who in the end would get to wear her coronet.

Diane had something bulky over her arm. For a second I thought it was the mermaid dress, though I'd seen her leave that in the back of Tom's car. Then I saw she was holding the big dark brown beach towels that the twins keep in their car.

I put on Mike's jacket and went carefully across the moss green rocks, trying to stay in the slice of light made by someone's extra-bright headlights.

"Elisa?" I called softly.

Scooter was perched on a rock a few feet from the edge but Elisa still stood, bent over, staring down into the water. She didn't move when I called her name, and neither did Scooter.

I went as close to her as I dared, moving silently,

saying her name over and over so I wouldn't startle her. "Elisa. Elisa, come sit with Mike and me." I took her arm. "Or come back and be with Scooter," I added.

She let me turn her and bring her with me.

Scooter was talking over his shoulder to Maria and her friends. Maria had some kind of coat draped over her bare shoulders.

"Tom and Grant will have to run at it," Scooter said. "If they don't, they'll never make it over the bulge. That bulge is a killer."

He spoke with the sureness of someone who's been there and knows, and Maria and her friends were paying close attention.

"It's going to be a trip for them, trying to see what they're doing," he added.

"Is there no way to get a light up there?" Maria didn't sound worried, just interested.

"Not in a hurry. We could have rigged something up if they'd planned it better." Scooter hung a seaweed crown in the crook of each elbow and stuck his hands in his pockets. "Man, that water's going to be ice when they hit it. And dark! Man, it's going to be blacker than black down there."

Elisa was making a strange sound, like Rusty Dog does when he's run too far and he's thirsty.

I put my arm around her shoulders.

I hadn't seen Mike since I started across the rocks, but now he was beside us carrying the blanket from his car. Even now, even in the middle of this, a glimpse of that blanket, its red tartan bright in the headlights, the smell of its itchy wool flashed me back to Murchisons, to the night we'd lain on it, and immediately I got that slipping-away feeling inside of me. For a second our eyes met, and again Mike smiled. "Remember?" that smile said.

"Here." He draped the blanket around Elisa's shoulders. She didn't help herself at all and it began sliding off. I wrapped it tightly around her, pulled one of her hands out from its folds, and said, "Here, hold it here."

I moved closer to Mike. "Thanks. But you must be freezing, too."

"I was hoping to share my jacket again," he whispered, and I opened the zipper and said, "Why not?"

We stood, Mike in front with his back to me. It wasn't as good a fit when we weren't facing, I thought, and it didn't feel as wonderful, either. But still, it was pretty nice, wrapped together in our warm cocoon.

To see the top of the Nail now I had to peer around him and that was fine, too. I could hide myself and not see anything if I didn't want to.

Someone began the chant, "Twinnies! Twin-nies!" and a few others took it up. "Nail it, twin-nies! Nail it!" But it wasn't as easy to yell at night. There was something awesome about that looming dark cliff, the lights whitening the base and the water below, the ominous blackness above.

"Do I see them?" someone called. I told myself I wouldn't look. But I did. The twins were dark figures silhouetted against the paler sky. They stood at the edge of the Nail, their shapes identical, their heads at the same angle. They could have been two of those stone figures you see pictures of, idols standing watch on Easter Island.

"Don't *say* they're not going to run at it." Scooter took his hands out of his pockets, slid off his rock, and stood up. Around us everything was hushed. The twins seemed to move a little. One of them bent over, maybe looking down.

Mike cupped his hands around his mouth and shouted. "Tom! Grant! Go back and run at it. It's the only way you'll make it."

I don't know if the words reached them before they jumped. They jumped outward, that I know, leaping forward like long jumpers trying to hit a mark.

I lost them then, the sky empty above them,

their falling bodies invisible against the dark cliff. When Scooter and Elisa had jumped, birds had flown, screeching, off the rocky ledges. But now it was as if some unknown hand had turned off sound and action. The twins fell silent and unseen. And then, close to the stem of the Nail, they appeared in the car headlights. Spotlights, I thought numbly. The twins were barefoot, wearing jeans. Tom, or maybe Grant, held his arms stretched above his head. Grant, or maybe Tom, was spread-eagled, as if he might hit facedown, and he almost did. But at the last second his feet came under him. There was an explosion of sound, a boom like a cannon, and water splashed up and over us, sloshing over the rocks and our feet. Tom and Grant had disappeared.

Around us were gasps, sighs, some cheering, voices, and someone wailing—Elisa! "She won't let them up. She won't!"

"You're a lunatic, Elisa," Scooter yelled. "Chill out, will you?"

"*You* chill out," I yelled back, and at that moment one twin's head bobbed up, like a seal's above the water.

"She's got the other one," Elisa screamed, trying to pull away from me. "She's keeping him." Tom or Grant was paddling water, looking for his brother, and then the second head broke the surface.

"Thank God," I whispered, knowing I'd been terrified myself, almost believing Elisa, almost expecting one of them never to appear again.

Tweeny gave a high little scream. "Oh, look at Grant's face!"

"It's Tom," Diane yelled. "Let me through." The crowd made a path for her the way they'd done on the floor of Spindrift.

I stared at Tom. Blood ran down his face. His head went underwater and when he came up again the blood had gone, only to start again, streams of it, thick as pencils running from the hairline down his face, flowing dark into the Deep.

TWELVE

TOM HAD TO HAVE twenty-seven stitches in his head. I was told the doctor at Mill Beach Hospital asked how it had happened, and Grant said Tom had fallen and hit his head on a rock. That was true, all right.

I wasn't there. No one went except Grant and Diane, who drove them in Betsy's car, which was easy to back out. Mike and Hopi donated their pants and shirts to the twins, since they were the closest in size, and wrapped themselves in the two brown towels.

"My, you could be a real Indian now," Tweeny told Hopi.

"Native American, Tweeny," Betsy corrected.

"Whatever. All he needs is a feather in his hair."

Hopi gave Tweeny a contemptuous glance. "I *am* a real Native American. It doesn't make any difference what I wear or what you call me."

At the hospital the doctors told Grant he looked

as if he were in shock, too, and Grant said he'd been terrified when he saw the gash that went across his twin's forehead from eyebrow to eyebrow.

We'd all been terrified.

They'd shaved his hair back and Scooter said he looked like a punk rocker. Scooter seemed to be enjoying everything immensely. I heard him say to Maria, "These things take planning. You don't just jump off the Nail the way you'd jump off a curb."

"You sure planned your jump well," Maria said.

"And did it well!" Scooter put one of the seaweed wreaths back on his head, and I thought, If he puts the other one on Maria I'll pluck his eyes out. But he didn't.

"You were so brave," Diane told Tom lovingly. "I've never seen anybody so brave."

Blood flowed down Tom's face, dripped onto Mike's pale shirt, and Betsy, who said she knew what to do, wadded up a white sweatshirt that someone provided and held it to his forehead. "These are the pressure points," she said. "Push with your fingers here and here."

"Oh, she's a medical doctor, too," Scooter said, but we were all glad to have someone do something.

"You were so brave," Diane said again, and

Tom's mouth twisted in what might have been a smile.

"Give us a break," Mike said. "Okay, he was brave, but more than that, he was dumb. He might have been killed."

No one paid any attention.

Elisa stood away from all of us, folded in the tartan blanket, staring out across the ocean. Scooter called her name once, then shrugged and made a face when she didn't turn.

"We should probably try to get that blanket for Tom," Mike whispered. "But I think maybe Elisa needs it more than he does."

"Let's all keep our mouths shut about what happened here," Scooter yelled. "If they find out, it'll be the end of the jumping."

I filed that thought away to consider later.

Mike and I had driven Tweeny and Betsy up to the top of the Nail to get the twins' car. The headlights were still on, shining blindingly into the darkness of space, and it was the way I'd imagined it. Only worse.

I couldn't seem to stop trembling as Mike drove me home. I'd tried to convince Elisa to let us take her, but she'd just shaken her head and said, "I have to go with Scooter."

"This will be an end of the jumping, anyway, won't it?" I asked Mike, forcing the words out between my clenched teeth.

"I doubt it," Mike said. "Hopi will jump. Maybe some of his friends, too. Getting your head ripped apart's not bad enough to stop them. It only adds to the prestige. Things haven't gone far enough yet."

"You mean someone's got to die?" I asked. "Has everybody gone crazy, including us? We've got to tell somebody about this, Mike. The police?"

"There's a fine for jumping now," Mike said. "That doesn't stop anybody. And the police can't sit out here, waiting to catch someone in the act. Everything's too wide open."

"We could tell in time to stop Hopi," I urged.

"I hate to be a nark," Mike said, "but you're right. This is too serious to let alone."

"Remember that nice police officer who came to school last year? What was his name? Stacy? Something like that? Remember? He was with the drug prevention program. We could find out who he was."

"That's an idea," Mike said. "Let's think about it."

Usually, when we get to my house, Mike walks

me to the porch. Tonight he didn't. "If your dad looked out the window and saw me wearing nothing but a towel he might chase me with his shotgun," Mike said.

I smiled. "My dad doesn't have a shotgun."

So we kissed and hugged briefly in the car, and Mike waited till I was safely inside. I waved, then closed and locked the door. The hall clock said three minutes to midnight but someone was still up. The living room lights were on and I heard Johnny Carson's voice on the television. Rusty Dog came padding through from the kitchen, wagged his tail sleepily, and went back. I was debating whether to just call good night and slip quietly upstairs when Mom shouted, "Dru, honey? Is that you? Come in for a second."

I took a deep breath and told myself to stay cool, to act as if tonight had been nothing more than an ordinary happy time at Spindrift. My mother was certainly not the one to unload on.

As soon as I got to the living room door she sprang up from where she'd been sitting on the couch and took my hands. "Did you have a fun time, baby?"

My lying eyes smiled into hers. "Oh yes. Lots of fun. Has Dad gone to bed?"

She nodded. "Yes. Can you sit for a minute? Here." She went back to the couch and patted the place beside her. "Turn off the TV first, will you?"

I did, then sat on the very edge of the couch cushions to show I would only be here for a minute.

"Dru, I have something to tell you." Mom smiled widely at me and I thought I'd never seen her look younger or happier. She was wearing her silky pink summer robe and her cheeks were the same soft, glowing color. Her hair hung loose around her shoulders.

"It must be something great, huh?" I smiled back at her. "You sold that condominium?"

"Oh, no such luck." Mom rolled her eyes. "They want to think about it and look it over again tomorrow. Can you imagine? Some people! No, it's better than that."

"You sold a million-dollar house? You *bought* a million-dollar house?"

She shook her head. "Dru! No, nothing to do with real estate. At least not *my* real estate." She paused. "Tomorrow night we are invited to dinner at El Nido."

"Dinner? At Mike's house?" I was stunned. "But why? We hardly know them. I mean, you hardly know his parents and . . ."

"Well, we *did* meet that time, you know, at the restaurant."

Oh, I knew all right. "Are you a ballet dancer?" Mike had asked, looking at me, seeing me for the first time. I remembered.

"Well?" Mom's eyes sparkled. "So?"

I was speechless.

It didn't matter. Mom was rattling on. "Flora called me this evening. She apologized that it was such short notice. 'Spur-of-the-moment thing,' she said. It seems Sam suggested we get together."

Sam, Mike's dad, who'd said to Mom, "You're as lovely as ever, Connie."

"They don't know too many people yet in La Paloma . . ."

"But Sam lived here, didn't he?" I asked. "*He* knows people."

"He was just a teenager when he left, Dru. Everything's changed. They haven't had time to socialize much as a family. That's how Flora put it. And since, well, since Sam and I knew each other, my gosh, we've known each other since kindergarten, and now you and Mike are such an item . . ."

Mom stopped to breathe.

I picked up the newspaper that lay on the coffee table, rolled it into a tube, and tapped it against my leg. "What does Dad say?"

Mom groaned. "Oh, you know what an old stick-in-the-mud he is."

"I don't know that at all," I said, angry and defensive. "You mean he doesn't want to go, so that makes him a stick-in-the-mud?"

"He hates parties. But he'll go."

"Is this a party?"

"I didn't mean that. It's just the three of us and Flora, Sam, Mike, and the little girl. What's her name?"

"Janie," I said.

Mom took the paper from me and gripped my hands. "Honey, I'd really like to go." She glanced around the living room. "I'd never be able to ask them back here, of course. But we could take them to the Marvue. They must like it there. It would be expensive, but we'd get your father's discount. And oh, sweetie, aren't you just *dying* to see what the ritziest house in town looks like inside?"

"Well . . ." I knew I did want to see how El Nido looked inside. Not because it was the ritziest house in town but because it was where Mike lived. He'd asked me a couple of times, after school, and once he'd said, "Janie's dying of curiosity about Dru."

I'd smiled and put him off. Of course I wanted

to see his home. But something about going to El Nido scared me. Maybe later, when I was more sure of myself, and Mike. But now we were all going—my whole family. I'd see where he ate dinner, the chairs he sat in, maybe even his bedroom . . . only if we got a tour, of course. And afterward, lying in bed at night, I'd be able to imagine . . .

"See?" Mom said gleefully. "You want to, too." Her voice lowered. "You know something else, Dru. I think this is a sign that Mike's serious about you. I bet he told his parents that, and Flora and Sam thought it might be a neat idea to get to know you."

"Oh, Mom!"

Rusty came padding in from the kitchen, probably to see why we still weren't in bed at this late hour. He gave a giant yawn, clambered up on the couch beside me, and put his head on my lap. I stroked his ears.

"Well, Mom," I said. "I guess you accepted."

"Are you serious? I accepted with pleasure. You can wear . . ." Mom stopped. "Dru. I've just noticed. Your sandals are soaking wet. And what is that green stain on your skirt?"

I brushed at the mark, spreading it more. "Mike

and I were walking on the beach by Spindrift and climbing over some rocks," I said.

Mom smiled. "I know. I remember when Sam and I went on dates. There was no Spindrift then, of course, but . . ."

I couldn't take this reminiscing. Not tonight. "How come you never go on like this about your dates with Dad?" I asked.

Mom smiled and touched my cheek. "Oh, but I do. Haven't I told you about the night I first saw him, playing the piano? The way he watched me so seriously with those sea blue eyes? And the night we rented the gondola in Venice—Venice, California—and how your father pretended to take the moon and hang it on the bow? Haven't I told you?"

"Yes," I said.

I lifted Rusty's head and shooed him down off the couch. "Mom, I'm really tired. I can't stay up another minute."

"I know." Mom leaned forward and gave me a hug. "Don't worry about me and your father. We have our ups and downs, but we love each other." She crossed her heart with a finger. "I mean it. Honest."

I smiled at her, feeling better. Probably when

an old boyfriend came out of the past it was kind of exciting and interesting.

"Go to bed, honey," Mom said. "Sleep well. Have delicious dreams."

There were no delicious dreams for me and not much sleep, either. I'd known there wouldn't be. What dreams there were swirled with dark, falling bodies, blood, and now and then a mermaid in a dress of bright, shimmering green.

THIRTEEN

I HAD A PHONE CALL from my sister Claire the next day and one from Mike.

Dad works Saturday mornings and Mom was showing the condo for the seventh time. She'd said she'd be home to eat lunch but after that she was going to Julie's Beauty Shop to have her hair and nails done. I was glad neither of my parents was around when Claire called. In our house privacy is hard to find.

Claire said New York was fine and her music was getting better and better, but she couldn't wait to come back to La Paloma in August when summer school ended. "What's up at home?"

I told her about the jumping. "It's like some kind of disease," I said. "The kind you can't stop once it starts."

"Don't you get hyped into doing it, Dru," she said sharply.

"Are you kidding? Not for a million bucks." I

was sitting on the bottom of the stairs and Rusty had come to sit next to me, his head on my lap.

Claire was silent. I stroked Rusty's ears.

"Suppose Mike decided to jump and he asked you to go with him?" she asked, and my heart began to beat awfully fast.

"In the first place *he* wouldn't jump. And in the second place he'd never ask me to do something I didn't want to do." I had one of those quick, sweet, backward flashes to Murchisons, quickly followed by Mike's voice. "Don't go. Don't go to Chicago." That came pretty close to asking me to do something I didn't want to do. But then he'd said he wasn't serious. So that didn't count. "What's more," I told Claire, "I wouldn't jump even if he asked me to."

"Oh, really?" Claire sounded amused. "Well, what if Diane Skoal offered to take your place? Then would you consider jumping with Mike?"

"This is the dumbest conversation we've ever had," I said, rubbing Rusty's head so furiously that he decided to move away and lie on the hall rug. "And I don't want to talk about it anymore, either."

"Okay by me," Claire said. "So what else is going on?"

"Not much. Except tonight we're going to the

Moriartys' for dinner. The whole family." I listened to my bombshell drop.

"My, my," Claire said at last. "Mom must be thrilled. And Dad?"

"I think he's okay."

"And you?"

"Scared out of my mind. I hope Mom doesn't get too crazy, you know the way she does when she's nervous? She can be so embarrassing. Twittery."

"I know. Gushy." Claire was quiet for a second. "This guy's really important to you, isn't he?"

I nodded. "Yes."

"Stay calm, little sister," Claire said gently. "Call me tomorrow."

"Okay."

We blew phone kisses the way we always do before we hang up.

Without disturbing Rusty I called Elisa, but there was no answer. Then I called Lizzie before I remembered she and her parents had left early to drive to Long Beach. Tomorrow was her grandparents' anniversary.

Mike had spent the morning on one of the building sites with his dad. Mom was home when he called, the condo still unsold. She gave me a sly smile when I said, "Hello, Mike," and even closed the kitchen door between us when I carried the phone on its long cord into the hall.

"I hear we're having company at our house for dinner," he said.

"Did you have anything to do with the invitation?" I asked.

"I'm as surprised as you are. But pumped up. Definitely pumped up."

"My stomach hurts," I said.

"Naw!"

I asked Mike if he'd heard how Tom McInerney was and he said he was doing okay. The doctor had told him if he'd hit those rocks any harder when he fell he'd have had a split skull and been taken to the morgue instead of the hospital.

I shivered. "Mike?" I lowered my voice even though the kitchen door was closed and I could hear Mom clattering dishes. "We've got to tell, fast."

"I almost told my dad this morning," Mike said, "but I'm not sure he's the right one. We may not have a chance to talk about it tonight but . . ."

"Oh, not tonight," I said. "Please. Tonight I'll have enough to handle. Tomorrow."

Mom came tiptoeing out of the kitchen, squeezed past me on her way upstairs, appeared again a few minutes later on the top step, an outfit in each hand. She held them high.

"I have to go now," I told Mike. "Bye. See you tonight."

"Wear your hair that way . . . you know," Mike said.

I smiled. "I know."

Mom came on down the stairs. "I hope I didn't mess up your phone call. My beauty shop appointment's in fifteen minutes and I want your opinion. Which one for tonight? This?" "This" was her white linen dress still in its plastic bag from the cleaners. "Or this?" "Or this" was the silky red suit with the slit in the skirt that she'd bought in Loehmanns' back room.

"The dress," I told her and she nodded.

"Classy yet casual. You think it's casual enough?"

"You'll be beautiful," I said.

"And you'll wear your blue cotton, won't you? The one you wore to my birthday dinner?"

"Yep!" I pulled my eyes down and the corners of my mouth up and stuck out my tongue. "I'll be beautiful, too."

Mom laughed. "Oh, you!"

"Your dad has that nice Brooks Brothers' shirt and I thought his blazer . . ."

"Definitely his blazer," I agreed.

"It's going to be so neat," Mom said.

My stomach rolled anxiously, as if I were on a small boat in big surf. Should I ask her to behave tonight? Was that the kind of thing you could ask your mother? Oh, if only Mike and I were going out, just the two of us. To Spindrift. No, somewhere far from Spindrift—somewhere in Vista del Mar maybe, where we'd dance and kiss and be in love.

Mom was leaving so I waved good-bye, then tried to call Elisa's house again. There was still no answer so I went into the living room and lay on the couch. Rusty came, and I lifted one of his lollopy ears so I could whisper, "I really do want to go to Chicago, you know. I do. I won't let anything stop me."

He stared at me skeptically.

"I think we need a run," I told him, and I changed into my Nikes and shorts and he and I set off. It was a gorgeous afternoon. Sailboats raced, their sails seeming to overlap as they rounded the buoy. Kids splashed in the soapsud shallows.

I saw a man, fully clothed, sleeping behind a rock, his possessions beside him in two grocery bags, the beach around him strangely empty. I remembered Virginia saying, "Nobody ever stops to talk to me." So sad! But even if the man had been awake I knew I wouldn't have gone near him.

Up on the cliff was El Nido.

Tonight we'd be there.

I ran faster, poor Rusty puffing to keep up. We pounded through a pile of seaweed, and a swarm of little sand flies rose to dart around my face. Oh, Elisa! I hope you're all right. What did you do with that awful crown? I hope you dropped it in the garbage with the boot. I hope you didn't hang it up in your room, the smell filling the air, reminding you. Oh, Elisa! I hope you didn't do that!

FOURTEEN

WE DROVE UP the narrow, winding road to El Nido, Mom worrying constantly whether the white linen dress was a bad choice, whether it would be creased by the time we got there. She'd look tacky all evening. She half stood, smoothing the dress under her, trying not to put her weight on it.

"Sit down and don't be silly," Dad said in a reasonable voice. "If it's creased they'll know it's linen, the real, classy stuff." He gave me a wink in the driver's mirror.

Mom's nervousness should have been contagious, but Dad seemed calm enough. I didn't know what I felt—scared, excited, uptight.

The views of ocean and beach got more spectacular the higher we climbed. Bougainvillea tangled purple and scarlet on either side of the road, and birds sang their end-of-day songs. I told myself to stay calm.

"There's going to be a beautiful sunset," Dad

said, and I saw how deep a blue the sky was over the ocean, the sun dipping red toward the horizon.

There was a flagged courtyard in front of the house and a stone fountain, its dish held up by two long-legged bronze birds. Water spilled like magic.

Mom pointed. "The nest," she whispered, "El Nido."

"The eggs are going to get wet," Dad whispered back.

Palms fanned their great leaves against the white walls and there were clumps of ferns and birds of paradise.

"Definitely owner occupied," I told Mom.

We were standing outside the car, Mom smoothing the wrinkles from her skirt, when the carved front door opened and there they were, Mr. and Mrs. Moriarty, Mike, and Janie.

"So nice you could come." That was Mrs. Moriarty, also in a white dress, but with a pleated skirt and no wrinkles.

"So nice of you to invite us." That was Mom.

The men shaking hands.

Mike smiled at me, then took my hand, holding on to it, swinging it between us as we walked toward the door. Already I felt better.

"Lovely evening."

"Lovely breeze."

"Lovely view."

The adults talked politely. Janie ran up and took Mike's other hand, timing it to swing along with ours.

And then we were inside, in the cool whiteness of El Nido.

I could never have imagined it. At first there was nothing but impressions. Of great stretches of blond wood floors that curved around the white walls. Of windows filled with sky and sea and faraway cliffs and headlands.

"How about something cool to drink?" Mr. Moriarty asked, and his wife led the way into a room that seemed made of glass. There was wicker furniture with yellow cushions. A tray with a pitcher and glasses ringed with yellow waited on a wicker table.

I stood with Mike, looking down on my beach, where earlier I'd run with Rusty Dog. How strange. From here it looked so different. The beach cottages could have been dollhouses; the sailboats I'd seen racing earlier, toy boats.

Janie tugged at my dress and pointed to her feet. She was wearing little sandals with cutouts, just like mine.

Mike laughed. "I filled Janie in on what wonderful taste you have," he said.

"I should have worn mine tonight," I told Janie. "And I like your skirt."

She stuck her hands in the sunflower pockets and smiled shyly at me.

Afterward, there were other impressions to sort through. Mike's mother, her dark hair short and neat, her eyes the same blue as her son's. Mike's dad, boisterous and healthy looking, letting Janie crawl all over him on the wicker couch, tossing her in the air. No outward sign of the massive heart attack or the triple bypass. He looked as if he'd never been sick a day in his life.

But for me, the night and the house were filled with Mike. Mike sprawled in a big white chair, Mike smiling at me, our fingers touching as he refilled my glass of juice.

The dinner was delicious—a chicken salad with almonds that Janie picked out and ringed around her plate.

"You don't like almonds?" I asked.

She shook her head, wispy blond hair flying. "Uh-uh. They're yukky. They're like teeth."

She leaned close and crooked a finger at me so she could whisper. "Are you and Mike going to get married?" Then drew back to watch me, bright-eyed as a little bird.

I could feel Mike's amused glance and my own

face getting warm. I crooked a finger at her so I could whisper back. "It's too soon to know."

She nodded, then motioned me close again. "I like you better than Diane."

I nodded. "Good." But I felt as if ice water had been thrown on me. Janie knew Diane. Diane had been here. For dinner? I couldn't imagine the Moriartys inviting every girl of Mike's to dinner. I'd thought this was because of the old-acquaintance thing. Face it, I'd also thought it was because I was special.

"Mike tells us you're off to Northwestern in the fall," Mrs. Moriarty said.

"Yes."

"Good for you."

I took a delicate bite of chicken, aware of her intent gaze.

"And did Mike tell you that his old mother is starting school again in the fall, too?"

"You?" I asked.

She nodded. "I've signed myself up for some classes. I never finished, you know. I met Mike's dad and we got married and I dropped out and . . ."

"Uh-oh, here it comes." Mr. Moriarty screwed up his face.

"And it was something I always regretted," Mrs.

Moriarty went on. "Not marrying Mike's dad, of course." She gave him a fond smile. "That was the best thing I ever did. But not finishing college. You need to have your own life, if you're a woman *or* a man. A degree helps give you choices."

Mr. Moriarty pretended to play a violin and made a humming noise. "Oh, the sad story."

"It's true and you agree with me."

I heard a flash of irritation in his wife's voice.

"I never went to college and I did okay," Mr. Moriarty chirped, and I had a feeling this wasn't a new argument.

"Oh, Sam," Mom agreed. "You did marvelously." She waved her fork. "Look at all this. You turned out to be such a . . . such a tycoon." I bent my head over my plate. Don't chatter, Mom. Don't gush.

"Still, I think it's a good idea for Mike to get himself a business degree," Mr. Moriarty said. "His mother planned it this way. I get Mike in the business with me right away so he can start learning, and at the same time he's working toward that B.S."

"It may take a while," Mike said.

His mother nodded. "It will. But you have a while."

"If you *are* going to college, though, everybody says you can't beat the California system," Mike said, looking straight at me.

Dad put down his fork. "I agree. But Connie and I were happy that both our daughters got good scholarships, even though they are far away. Claire has so much musical talent and Dru such a gift for languages. The scholarships make it possible for us, financially." It was a strangely personal thing for Dad to say and yet there was dignity in it. Oh, Dad, I thought, I love you so much. He raised his iced-tea glass to me and then to Mike and said, "It's nice to know that whatever regrets we adults have, our children won't need to have them."

Everyone was suddenly looking at everyone else and I had a sense of important issues discussed and decided. I sensed Mrs. Moriarty's relief and the genuine warmth when she smiled at me.

She leaned across the table toward Dad. "Did you know Sam and I heard you play at the restaurant one night when we were having dinner? You are a wonderful musician. Will you play for us later? Or is that like having a doctor in your home and asking her to diagnose your condition?"

Dad laughed. "It's not like that at all. I'm always happy to play."

And he did, afterward, with the moon hanging outside the open curve of window, lamplight falling on the shining black surface of the piano. He played the kind of music he plays on weekends in the restaurant and then, so unobtrusively that everything melded together, he moved into the "Moonlight Sonata," the notes falling pure and white in the whiteness of the room.

I looked at my father sitting there and it wasn't hard to see why Mom had fallen in love with him. And I looked at her, at the dreaminess on her face, and I knew it was true. She loved him still.

I turned my head and Mike was watching me, his eyes serious. Janie had cuddled in the big white chair beside him and I thought she might be asleep.

"Enough," Dad said. He ran his fingers in a trickle of notes over the keys and stood up. He seemed comfortable and totally at ease and I thought of all the luxury hotels he'd played in over the years. A startling thought came to me. My dad is a sophisticated man. My father.

"That was lovely," Mrs. Moriarty said. "Truly lovely."

"You have a big talent there, my friend," Mr. Moriarty said. "We knew that the first time we heard him, didn't we, Connie? You were so impressed you up and took after him, and left me standing with egg on my face."

"Poor baby. And you hate eggs," his wife said lovingly, and everybody laughed, and suddenly it was almost a joke, one of those things that hurt at the time but that make a good story later.

I didn't get to see Mike's room after all. Janie took me to hers so I could visit her rabbits and her hamster, whose name was Daniel Johnson.

"Where did you get *that* name?" I asked her.

"I made it up," she said.

Mrs. Moriarty didn't suggest we see the rest of the house, and my mom didn't ask. That wasn't like her, and I was grateful.

Before we left, Mike and I walked around the stone-flagged terrace to the low wall that divided the grounds from the harsh cliff beyond. Janie had gone unwillingly to bed and we were alone.

Below us the beach was dark except for the lights in the cottage windows, and the flames rising from one of the fire rings. The sea stretched dark, past the horizon, into the sky.

"Do you know the top of the Nail is almost this high?" Mike asked suddenly.

I peered over the wall. "So awful!"

"I've been trying to remember that officer's

name, you know, the one we talked about," Mike said. "It's Officer Tracy."

"Sure. I remember now. The kids called him Dick Tracy."

"He wasn't too uptight," Mike put in.

"Not a bit. And he was tough," I said. "He'd be perfect. Let's call him tomorrow and see if we can talk to him."

"Tomorrow's Sunday," Mike said.

"I know. But police officers can't take Sundays off. Robbers don't."

"Or burglars," Mike added, putting his arms around me, kissing my nose.

"Or murderers." I kissed his chin.

We smiled at each other.

"What will we say?" I asked.

"Just tell him the truth, I guess. Tell him something awful is going to happen if it's not stopped."

"I think we should have done it before. But it's so hard. Why is it so hard, Mike?"

"Because these are our friends and we think we're smart enough to handle it ourselves."

I hugged Mike tight. "But we're not. And you know what? Tomorrow this big, humongous . . . humongous secret will lift right off me. Oh, it's going to feel so good!"

"I'll call you early in the morning," Mike said.

"We'll decide what time we should go. Actually, we'll probably have to call him and set up an appointment."

I nodded.

He pressed his cold cheek against mine. "Do you know how hard it was for me tonight, not to rush at you and kiss you like this . . . and like this?"

"Do you know how hard it was for me?"

"Oh, Dru."

"Oh, Mike." We were laughing and serious at the same time.

"Whatever was said at dinner, I still wish you weren't going away," Mike said.

"I wish it, too. I don't know how I'm going to bear it."

"Don't then," Mike said, "because I can't stand it, either."

We stood, our foreheads touching, our fingers entwined.

"You're asking me to jump," I said. "Think about it, Mike. There are all kinds of jumps."

"No—I'd never . . ." He stopped. "Dru? Am I doing that?"

"Yes, and I don't want you to. It's so hard already."

We heard the others coming then, my mother

marveling at the view, Mr. Moriarty telling Dad how they'd had to blast the cliff top to get level ground to build on, and Mike and I moved apart.

Before we left, Mrs. Moriarty served cappuccino in little eggshell cups, and we thanked them for inviting us. Mom said how we'd love to have them as our guests at the Marvue some night before I left, and Mr. Moriarty said, "Great! And maybe Andy will play for us again."

We didn't talk much on the way home. Once Dad asked, "Did you enjoy everything, Connie?" and Mom said, "Oh, yes. It was wonderful." Then she added, "I'm sorry I wore this dress, though. What a disaster. I mean, a person can't keep standing the whole night!"

But I thought she said it in an absentminded way, as if she was thinking about something else, something important. Once she turned around to look at me, not speaking, just pulling on her lower lip.

That's why I wasn't that surprised when she came into my room later. Although it was past midnight I wasn't asleep.

"Dru? Are you awake?"

"Sure." I made room so she could sit beside me.

"Honey, I'd never advise you to do anything I

didn't think was right. You know that? Dru, we understand college is important. But that boy is in love with you. The way he watches you. The look in his eyes. And you're in love with him, too."

I started to speak but she put her fingers against my lips. Her hand smelled of the apple-blossom lotion she uses.

My heart had started to beat fast.

"Those feelings are going to dim if you separate. Absence doesn't make the heart grow fonder, Dru. It makes it forget. Do you want to lose Mike to some other girl?"

The image of Diane slid into my mind and I tried to slide it back out.

Mom plucked nervously at my sheet. "I would never have married Sam Moriarty, because I didn't really love him. I love your dad and I hope you understand that. But for you it's different. Anyone can see you and Mike are crazy about each other."

"But, Mom—"

"It would be a great life for you with him, Dru. I'm not only talking about the house and the money and the business. That's part of it, of course. But for you there's love, too."

"Mom! We're eighteen years old!"

"So? I'm talking about the rest of your lives." Her voice was urgent. "Dru, don't go to Chicago."

"You mean I should give up my scholarship, stay here, hang around, wait for Mike?"

"No. What's to stop you going to San Diego State, too? Go with him."

"I'd never get in this quarter. And you'd have to pay tuition and books . . . and a place for me to live."

"You're working for the rest of the summer, anyway. You could save something and we'd manage. Maybe you could drive down with Mike. Or we could think about getting you a little used car. Then you could drive to San Diego every day. It's not that far . . . only an hour, an hour and a half."

"Mom!" I turned my face to the wall. "Stop it. You're asking me to change all my plans because it's too risky to leave Mike here alone. It's hard enough for me to be strong."

"That's how a lot of girls lose a lot of guys," Mom said.

I felt the bed move slightly as she got up.

"I want you to have the love I've had with your dad . . . but more. There's nothing wrong with money and security to ease your way in life, honey."

I sensed her there in the pink summer robe, smelling of apple blossoms, but I didn't turn around.

"I thought you wanted a good education for me. And other things to come later. I thought we talked about that at dinner tonight. I got a scholarship, Mom. It's important. Mike's only going to school part-time. I'd slack off. I might never finish. That happens to a lot of girls, too."

I heard her sigh. "You could lose him, Dru," she whispered.

I heard the door close and she was gone. But what she'd said stayed in the room, moving restlessly in my mind.

FIFTEEN

THE PHONE RINGING downstairs woke me up. All around me the house had that before-dawn feeling, nobody stirring, the light coming pale through my drapes. Still groggy with sleep I looked at my bedside clock. Ten minutes past five. What? Who?

I sat up and tried to focus. Last night . . . Mike and I'd agreed to go to the police. But this early? My heart gave a giant thud. Maybe something was wrong with my sister? I got out of bed tripping over the sandals I'd kicked off last night.

Below, Dad was already talking to someone on the phone, Mom beside him. "Dru?" Dad called. "It's Elisa's mother. She's worried. She wants to talk to you."

"Elisa's mother?" I repeated, racing down the stairs. "Hi, Mrs. Fratello."

"Dru? Do you know where Elisa is? She didn't come home last night."

"No. Uh-uh." I ran my fingers through my hair. "Wait, I called her at—"

Mrs. Fratello interrupted. "She and I went to the gas company because they'd overcharged . . ." She stopped, as if realizing none of this mattered.

"Was she all right then?"

"She said she was tired. But she's been tired a lot lately. She sat in the car with her eyes closed. I had to be at work at five and she asked if she could drive me and keep the car, and pick me up at midnight when I finished, and I said okay. But she never came. Vesta, you know, the hostess, drove me home. I was pretty mad." She paused. "But I never feel right till Elisa's in, so I lay down on the couch to wait . . ."

Her voice was breaking, and I said quickly, "Oh, Elisa probably stayed over with someone, that's all."

"I fell asleep," Mrs. Fratello said. "I didn't wake up till after four this morning and I made myself wait till five to call you and Lizzie in case she had slept over with one of you."

"Uh-uh," I said. "And Lizzie's in Long Beach."

In the kitchen I heard the sound of the coffeepot being filled.

Mrs. Fratello's voice hardened. "Do you think Elisa's with that Scooter?"

I remembered Tom McInerney saying, "She'd do anything for Scooter," and I spoke in a rush. "All night? I doubt it."

"She seemed so much better when she was with him—in the beginning. The depression seemed to go—all of that. But lately . . ." She stopped. "Do you know how I can reach him, Dru? I don't even know his last name."

"Navarro," I said. "Listen, I'll call him for you and get back to you in a few minutes."

It was twenty past five. I found the Navarros' phone number and called. So what if his parents were mad! It served them right for having Scooter for a son. The phone rang and rang and rang. I redialed. On the twelfth ring a man answered, his voice so loud and irritable that I had to hold the phone away from my ear. "What is it?"

"May I speak to Scooter, please?"

His rage pulsed out at me. "Do you know what time it is, young lady?"

"It's an emergency," I said.

"What do you mean, an emergency?" His voice was slightly less grumpy.

"One of his friends didn't come home last night."

He snorted. "Is that all?"

I was standing there and I didn't know what I was hoping. That Scooter hadn't come home, either, which might mean Elisa and he were off doing something stupid, but not necessarily dangerous. Of course, with Scooter you never knew.

"Hold on and I'll get Sydney."

Sydney? Scooter was Sydney. And he was at home.

I hung on to the silent phone. Mom brought me a glass of orange juice, but I shook my head. And then I heard Scooter's voice. "Who is it?"

"Dru."

"Oh." He sneezed.

"God bless," I said automatically, though actually I didn't care if God blessed him or not. "Elisa didn't come home last night."

"Well, I don't know where she is," he said. "I didn't even *see* her yesterday."

"How come? You see her every day."

"Yeah, well, not yesterday."

"You didn't go out with her last night?"

There was a pause. "No. I was with somebody else. Not that it's any of your business."

I guessed it was Maria. She'd dangled those earrings and who knew what else at him and he'd dropped Elisa and gone to her.

Scooter lowered his voice confidentially.

"Elisa's totally wacko, you know. Seeing things, hearing things. She's getting to be Miss Ultradrag."

I waited while he blew his nose before I said, "I hope your cold turns into pneumonia and you die a lingering death," and banged down the phone. My father, who was leaning against the banister listening and drinking his coffee, jumped and spilled coffee on the rug. "You like Scooter that much, huh?" he asked.

I closed my eyes. "Yuck! What a cockroach! And now I have to call Elisa's mother, and I don't know what to say. Dad? Do you think she should tell the police?"

"Yes. They can check in case there's been an accident."

Mrs. Fratello answered right away and Dad talked to her. Then I spoke to her again, though she was crying and I'm not sure if she understood or even heard.

"Mrs. Fratello, I'm going to call a friend of mine. We'll go looking for Elisa, too. I know the places she hangs out. If she was tired, she just might have pulled off the road somewhere and gone to sleep in the car."

"Thanks, Dru."

"Please, please try not to worry." But of course she'd worry. I was worrying.

After I'd called Mike, and while I waited for him to come, Mom tried to force me to eat a piece of toast and drink a glass of milk, but I couldn't get it down. I had this terrible thought and it wouldn't go away. Elisa wouldn't! She wouldn't. It was the first thing I said to Mike when he came. "It's not that I think she'd actually jump, Mike. It's just the way she kept looking down into the Deep yesterday. And she has been sort of . . . obsessed with it. But I'm sure she wouldn't jump. She's too scared."

"Maybe we should cruise by the Nail first and, you know, just check, anyway." Mike didn't quite look at me, but he put his hand over mine for a second before he turned the car toward Coast Highway.

I filled him in on my talk with Scooter. "He was with Maria, I know it," I said. "And I'm trying to be glad. It'll be better for Elisa in the end, but she's going to be so hurt for a while."

The closer we got to the Nail the more my heart pumped. Silly, I told myself. Melodramatic. Quit it!

Mike stopped the car just inside the opening to the meadow and we looked across its emptiness to the edge of the cliff. One glance showed us that there was no car there.

I slid down in my seat. Thank you, God. Thank you.

"What kind of a car does Elisa's mom have, anyway?" Mike asked as he swung around and edged us back to the highway.

"A blue Pontiac with white primer patches on the side."

"Let's go in on the path below and check," Mike said, and I knew suddenly that I'd been thankful too soon. He drove all the way to Mandela's rock. No car. The Deep lay sluggish and silent, untouched by sun. High on the cliff face I saw the ghostly white shapes of the gulls, huddled, headless, their necks tucked under their wings. "Do we need to get out?" Mike asked.

I shook my head, shivered. "Not when there's no car."

"Where next?" he asked, backing out the way we'd come.

"Let's try Kingfisher Cove. Elisa likes it there. She once told me she goes there when she's upset."

The Pontiac wasn't in the beach parking area at Kingfisher, and the cove was deserted except for a few sandpipers picking breakfast out of the shallows. The sun was just beginning to slant across the hills and warm the edges of the sand.

There was no blue Pontiac at the harbor where Lizzie and Elisa and I used to go to watch the fishing boats come in. A young guy in thigh-high rubber boots was hosing down the deck of the *Kitty Munroe*. I asked him if he'd seen a girl, pretty, with long red hair, and he splashed his hose into the water, grinned, and said, "Only in my dreams."

We cruised the streets of La Paloma. Twice we saw a police car cruising, too, and I wondered if we were all searching for the same blue Pontiac with the white primer patches.

"She could have just taken off," Mike said at last. "Sometimes, when things are bad enough, you just want to run."

I nodded. "Poor Elisa. Maybe she came to my house looking for me. Or she might have gone to Lizzie's. And neither one of us was home last night."

"Should we try Spindrift?" Mike suggested.

"It's not open till four."

"I know. But still. Where else is there?"

The serving area of Spindrift was closed up tight. Two or three gulls roosted on the picnic tables. A cat prowled behind the counter.

"I guess she's not here," Mike said, and then a voice spoke below us on the beach.

"*I'm* here. Come and talk to me."

I looked down and there was Virginia, sitting wrapped in her blanket, watching us.

"Oh, hi!" Mike jumped down the steps to the sand and I followed. "Hi, Virginia. We've lost a friend of ours. You didn't see her around, did you? She's got red hair down to here." He touched his chest.

"You mean the Queen of the Deep?" Virginia asked.

"What?" Mike sounded surprised.

"I saw the mermaid crown her the other night, didn't I?" Virginia asked. "The two of them got crowned. King and Queen of the Deep."

"That's right," I said. "That's the one." We were standing beside her now, looking down into her face, and I saw she wasn't any older than my mother. How sad that this was her life.

"Have you seen her since . . . since the night she became Queen?"

Virginia nodded. She fished a cotton square from her bag, opened it to reveal some broken bits of bagel. "Like a piece?" she asked.

"I just had breakfast," I said, and Mike shook his head. "Not now, thanks."

"When did you see her?" he asked.

"Last night. She was here on the beach, looking in through the glass and crying."

Fright moved cold inside of me. Probably Scooter and Maria had been there, dancing together, her earrings swinging. Maybe they'd even been kissing.

I crouched on the sand next to Virginia. "Did she say anything?"

"We talked some." Virginia scrabbled in her bag for a bottle of water, uncorked it, and took a sip.

"What did she say? What did you say? It's very important, Virginia."

"Let's see." She corked the bottle and balanced it on the sand. "I said, 'Don't cry, Queen of the Deep. Come down here. Come down and stay awhile and talk.'"

I sat back on my heels, my legs too weak to crouch any longer.

"She didn't even turn and look at me," Virginia said gloomily. "Hardly anybody does. Hardly anybody stops, either. Nobody wants to talk to me."

I hugged myself, shivering. Oh, it was cold here.

"You said she spoke, too," Mike said. "The Queen of the Deep. What did she say, Virginia?"

Virginia smiled. "She said, 'I'm coming.' But

she never did. She just ran along there." She waved toward the parking lot.

"Oh no, oh no!" I couldn't seem to stop saying "oh no." Virginia stared at me with interest, then Mike's arm was around me, helping me up, helping me across the sand to the parking lot, to his car.

"The same words the drowned girl said to her," I whispered. "Stay. Talk. Oh no, Mike. No."

"Do you want to go take another look?" he asked. "We don't have to. We could call the police."

"No," I said. "I want to go."

This time we drove all the way into the meadow. The wildflowers in the grass smiled up at the sun. The sky was a clean washed blue. It was a beautiful, beautiful day.

As soon as Mike stopped the car by the Danger sign we both saw the greasy, scarlet lines that crossed out the names Scooter Navarro and Elisa Fratello. The hearts were hidden under a scrawl of red.

I opened the car door. Something shiny lay on the grass. A lipstick tube, the top off, the scarlet lipstick only a stub. I thought this might be what a used bullet would look like, lying where someone had been shot. I picked it up.

"Is it hers?" Mike asked.

I sniffed its faint waxy perfume. "I don't know."

It was Mike who found the tire tracks that went right to the edge of the Nail and beyond.

We stood under the wide clear sky, the breeze blowing around us. And I was crying.

SIXTEEN

THE POLICE, when they came that awful morning, found Elisa's seaweed crown floating on the surface of the Deep, as quietly as the wreaths of gardenias would float there a week later at the memorial service. As peacefully as the small, carved wooden doll that Hopi brought to the service and laid on the water.

Divers tried for three days to get her body out of the car, the Pontiac shifting twice, sliding deeper into that sightless dark. It almost took a diver's life along with Elisa's as it went down, down, down, and in the end they had to leave it and her there.

Everybody has questions. I have one, such a small one in the immensity of what has happened. Had Elisa stood at the edge of the Nail and thrown her crown over before she got back in her mother's car and drove it off the cliff? Or had she worn it as she sat behind the wheel, the Queen of the Deep going to her Queendom? The trivial question nags and nags at me, and I know I'll never have an answer.

Just about all our old class came to the memorial service, even Scooter, wearing dark mirrored glasses and standing well to the back. I didn't look at him. I hope I never have to look at him again.

"It's not all his fault," Lizzie said one night when she slept over at my house and we lay talking till dawn. "Nobody forced Elisa to jump that first time. I can't figure out why girls do dumb stuff just because guys want them to. Anyway, it doesn't work."

"I know," I said. "And say people, not girls. Guys can be just as dumb." I was thinking of Tom McInerney at the memorial service, the healing gash a pink line across his forehead. Diane had been with him, restless Diane, turning once to smile over her shoulder at Hopi, touching Mike's shoulder as they left.

At least the Jumping the Nail craze is over. For this year. I guess I can't say it's over forever. As Claire says, there'll come another summer. Having her home this past month helped. Sometimes she or Dad played lovely tranquil piano concertos. And I could cry.

* * *

My flight to O'Hare was booked for Thursday. The night before I left, Mike and I went up to Murchisons. It felt like the end of summer, the pewter sky hiding the last of the sunset. Mike wrapped the tartan blanket around us; his lips and hands were cold.

"I love you, Dru," he said. "I wish you weren't going. But I know you have to."

"I'll be back," I said.

Elisa won't be.

Sometimes I imagine her down there with the other two drowned kids, tossing back her hair and laughing. "Well, you invited me and here I am. What will we talk about?"

But mostly I know that's not the way it is. I know she's dead when she should be alive, my friend Elisa, gone forever in the Deep.

Learning Center
Twin Groves Middle School
2600 N. Buffalo Grove Rd.
Buffalo Grove, IL 60089